BLOOD LIKE THE SETTING SUN

A MURDER ON MAUI MYSTERY

ROBERT W. STEPHENS

For my Felicia Dames

1

CHICKEN FINGERS AND PEEPING TOMS

Let me ask you a question. If you were trying to impress a beautiful young woman, would you take her to a chain restaurant - on Maui of all places? I didn't think so. I won't tell you the name of the restaurant in question because I'm about to say some derogatory things about it. However, I don't think it would be fair to not, at the very least, give you some clues. The name of the restaurant is two words. The first word starts with an *r* and the second starts with a *t*. In all fairness, I must disclose that I worked for one of this chain's Virginia locations while I was in school.

I believe everyone should be a waiter for at least six months. It educates you so much about society and the people you will encounter as you move through life. Most waiters develop their own theories about the ones they serve. I call my theory the rule of thirds. I realize this is also the name of a photography theory on what makes a pleasant shot composition. As an amateur photographer, and someone who has spent way too much money on all the gear, I can attest to being well aware of that theory. It's also the perfect name for my waiter theory, though, so forgive me for blatantly stealing it.

So here's how my theory goes. About one third of the population is comprised of people who are generally nice. They smile at you.

They're patient. They just have an overall attitude that says it's a good thing to help others and be kind to people. They almost always give you good tips since they're taking notice of how much you're running around to help them and others.

The second third of the population is generally indifferent to other people. It's not that they're rude or uncaring. They're just too wrapped up in their own lives and their own concerns to pay any attention to you. They consistently give you average tips.

I call the remaining third "the jerks." I usually employ a stronger word, but I don't want to offend sensitive readers. These are the types of people who speed up to intentionally block you after you put on your turn signal to move into their lane. If you're lucky, you only run into these people once or twice a week, but you see them several times a day when you wait tables. They take great pleasure in yelling at you, maybe because the fish they wanted to order wasn't caught that very morning. Really? Why would you go to a chain restaurant in a shopping mall if you are the type of food connoisseur who only eats fresh fish? Do you really think the Applebee's chef races down to the docks each morning just so he or she can purchase fresh fish that you can enjoy on your lunch break? I really don't know if this negative character trait is because they are ultimately unhappy with their own lives, or if there's simply a malfunction in a chromosome that creates these jerks. Note to any potential government managers reading this story, this third of the population makes for excellent IRS agents. This group will give you bad restaurant tips every time, even if you provide them with five-star service.

In addition to the mental frustrations of waiting tables, there's also the physical challenges the restaurant job places on you. The average waiter is on his or her feet around eight to twelve hours straight. It's pure hell on the knees and lower back. I bought an expensive pair of Rockport shoes when I first started the job. I still had discomfort at the end of my night, but the shoes helped to mini-mize it as much as possible.

We always had a meeting with the manager about fifteen minutes before each shift started. He or she would go over the special of the day, which was normally a food item they had too much of and were looking to unload. They would also consistently remind us to push alcohol sales. For those of you not familiar with the business, restaurants do not exist to sell you food. They are in the business of selling booze. The average mark-up on alcohol can be anywhere between 300 to 400 percent. Restaurants make far less profit on steaks, burgers, and pasta.

During one of these pre-shift meetings, the manager told us the restaurant had instituted a new policy. All wait staff were required to purchase specific shoes from the company. These shoes had a special rubber sole made by a company called Vibram. Supposedly, they would cut down on the slips, trips, and falls of the employees, which would in turn reduce the insurance premiums the company paid. I asked the manager why the company didn't give us the shoes for free instead of forcing us to pay for them. I know it was a naïve question from a less experienced version of myself, and I'm cringing as I admit that statement to you now. However, I was young and under the false impression the company should care enough about its employees and not ask a broke college student like myself to shell out forty-five dollars so the company could lower their workers' comp premium. I was immediately sent home for my insubordination and poor attitude. Later that night, as I sat in my bedroom, I noticed that my Rockports actually had Vibram soles. I couldn't believe my good luck. I returned to work the next night and showed my manager the soles, certain that I would be victorious in my battle of wills with the company. I'm sure you know what came next. He informed me that I could not wear my Rockports because they were black, and the company policy was that all staff were to wear brown shoes - never mind that I had already been wearing these same black shoes for over two years on the job and no one had ever said anything until now, including this particular manager. Bottom line: if I wanted to keep the job, I would need to shell out the money to buy the new company-approved shoes.

As I looked back on that conversation in the manager's office, which was tucked in the rear of the kitchen, I realized it was one of those defining moments we all have from time to time. These moments always appear out of the blue and we usually only have seconds to make a decision. Do we turn right or left? Are we in or are we out? Do we say, "Yes, I'll bow down to you almighty chain restaurant manager and buy the new brown shoes," or do we say, "Stick your brown shoes up your you-know-what?"

I'm sad to say that I chickened out that night and bought the shoes. I know it's not that massive of a defining moment, and it certainly didn't put me on some path to living a life of servitude and misery. And I don't mean to imply that it was any kind of big deal at all. I just want to tell you what was running through my mind as I drank a Coors Lite at the bar of this restaurant on Maui. It's strange how places can cause our minds to drift back to incidents we hadn't thought about for many years.

This place was thousands of miles away from the restaurant I worked at in Virginia, but it had the exact same décor and atmosphere as I remembered. It was ironic, too, that I was now having another defining moment in this restaurant. Many questions ran through my head. How had I gotten into this current predicament? What made me accept an assignment such as this? It was not what I had in mind when I agreed to work with Mara Winters.

So what exactly made me go to this establishment again after all of these years? I was on my first professional investigation. It certainly wasn't my first investigation, but it was the first one I had been paid for. For those of you who read my last tale, *Wedding Day Dead*, you'll probably remember that I was approached by a lawyer named Mara Winters. She offered to hire me from time to time to investigate sensitive matters for her clients. She represented many wealthy people with homes on the island, and she needed someone she could trust to not leak incriminating photos or details to the media.

This was my first case for her, and it involved following a cardiac surgeon, Dr. Theodore Peterson. Mara informed me that Teddy was fifty-two years old. He was my height, six-foot-two, but at 220 pounds, he outweighed me by twenty. He owned a second home in Wailea on the beautiful island of Maui. His main home was in Phoenix, where he lived with his wife, Karen Peterson, and his three children, age five to twelve.

I'd followed Dr. Peterson to the apartment of a young woman. She must have been watching for him because the door opened the moment he arrived, and she came bouncing outside. Bouncing was the key word. It was a sight to behold. She had quite the body on her, large breasts, a tiny waist, long blonde hair.

Dr. Peterson's next stop was the chain restaurant, which was located in the town of Kihei, a short and pleasant drive along the coast. I waited a few minutes after they entered the restaurant, and then I made my way over to the bar. I found a seat that offered an excellent view of Dr. Peterson and his beautiful young female friend. I didn't know who she was, but one thing was certain - she was not Mrs. Peterson. If I had to hazard a guess, I would say she was about twenty years younger than the forty-five-year-old wife of the good doctor. She giggled at every other sentence Dr. Peterson uttered. I wasn't close enough to tell whether she was putting on an act, but Peterson clearly ate it up.

According to my temporary employer, the Petersons vacationed on Maui a few times a year. Recently, however, Dr. Peterson had taken to visiting without his family. He claimed he was meeting friends for long weekends of golf, but Mrs. Peterson thought he was doing more than putting and driving. Judging by the dinner I was spying on, I had no doubt she was correct. I was told the Petersons had a prenuptial agreement that protected the doctor's millions, but it would be voided if he committed adultery. My employer wanted me to catch him in the act. I didn't think this dinner alone would be enough to convict him of cheating on his wife. I had no idea how I was going to accomplish my given task, short of sneaking up to the window of the doctor's home and praying I had an unobstructed view into his bedroom.

One of the things that made this assignment less than stellar was the guy who sat next to me at the bar. His name was Eddie, and he was attending a sales conference for a time-share company with a few properties on Maui. He looked like he was pushing fifty, which made his dinner selection a bit odd. You know of any guys his age who order chicken fingers and fries? He ordered a Long Island Iced Tea to go with it. The guy was strange. After his third drink, he asked me if I knew where he could find a girl for the evening. It took me a second to realize he was talking about a prostitute. To recap, this guy went to a chain restaurant. He ordered a meal typically designed for children, and he asked some random guy sitting beside him where he could hire a hooker. I informed this gentleman that I didn't know where precisely he could locate a companion, but I suggested he Google "escorts" or something like that. He thanked me profusely and stated he didn't know why he hadn't thought of that. I wanted to tell him it was probably because the strong drinks dulled his brain, but I decided it was best to smile and wish him good fortune and happy hunting.

I looked back to Dr. Peterson and his dining companion and saw he was paying the bill. They stood and left the restaurant a few minutes later. I followed at a discreet distance. I immediately realized I should have rented an average-looking car for the night. I drive a silver BMW Z3. It's not the most expensive car ever made, but it definitely isn't something that blends in with the crowd.

I'm just now realizing that I forgot to introduce myself. Forgive me. My name is Edgar Allan Rutherford. My parents, God rest their souls, were fans of the legendary mystery writer. The name Edgar was not an ideal name to grow up with. I was often the recipient of bullying on the playground. However, my friends started calling me Poe by the time I reached high school. Most people call me by that nickname now, but you may call me Edgar if you wish.

I moved to Maui several months ago after falling in love with the island and a police detective while visiting my best friend, Doug Foxx. The detective in question is named Alana Hu. She's half Hawaiian and half Japanese. To describe Alana as stunning would be the understatement of the century. She has long dark hair and a slender body that renders me speechless whenever I see her. Her dark eyes are her most enchanting feature, though. She and I tangled on a police investigation that prominently featured Foxx. To be more precise, he was arrested for the brutal murder of his girlfriend, Lauren, a famous and wealthy artist on Maui. Alana thought Foxx was guilty. I thought he was innocent. That disagreement naturally resulted in us butting heads. Nevertheless, I persuaded her it was better to date me than arrest me for interfering in a police investigation. Fortunately, she saw things my way.

It was ultimately my infatuation and undeniable attraction to Alana that was the deciding factor to sell my home in Virginia and relocate to Maui. I currently live with Foxx in the beautiful town of Ka'anapali, but I spend at least half the week at Alana's. Neither of us have committed to making the next move of officially living together. Maybe we're afraid to jinx a good thing.

But let's get back to my mission of catching Dr. Peterson in the act. I followed him to his beach house in Wailea. He owned a beautiful two-story pad on the coast. I already knew his address because his wife supplied it to the attorney who hired me. I had scouted it earlier in the day and learned I could easily approach it from the beach. There was a large bush near the back of the property that offered a good hiding place from which to stealthily watch the house. Fortunately for me, Dr. Peterson's young companion walked out to the large second-floor balcony that overlooked the ocean. My earlier characterization of her had been correct. She was a real looker. She wore a short cream-colored dress that showed off her toned legs and ample cleavage. Dr. Peterson joined her a few moments later. He had two martinis and gave her one. I watched them drink, talk, and laugh for several minutes. Peterson leaned forward and kissed her. He then took the empty glasses and placed them on a small round table beside two wooden chairs. He walked back to her and kissed her again.

I took a photograph of the kiss. Photography is a big hobby of mine, and I have a nice selection of pro-level lenses. I selected a fast 70-200mm lens. For those of you not in the know about lenses, a fast lens is a fancy way of saying it gives you the ability to shoot in lower light. They cost a hell of a lot more than regular lenses, but they're worth it. I checked the viewfinder on the back of my Canon and confirmed the photo had sharp focus and clearly showed Dr. Peterson's face. I debated how many more photos I needed to take to fulfill my work assignment. Before I could determine the answer, Dr. Peterson did something that shocked me. He bent the young woman over and removed her underwear. She leaned against the railing of the balcony as Teddy took her from behind. It took me a second to get over what I was actually seeing. Then I remembered why I was there, and I snapped several more photos of the sexual act.

Consider the prenuptial agreement null and void, Mrs. Peterson.

"Being a Peeping Tom is illegal. You know that, don't you?"

I was so startled by the voice behind me that I didn't immediately recognize who it was. Fortunately, I didn't drop my camera in the sand. I spun around and saw Alana looking at me. She had a huge smile on her face.

"Enjoying the view?" she asked.

"What are you doing here?"

"Teaching you a valuable lesson. Just because you're following someone doesn't mean someone isn't following you."

"How long have you been tailing me?"

"Since the restaurant."

"You were there?" I asked.

"At a table in the corner opposite you. How many drinks did that guy beside you have?"

"I lost count."

"You should increase your distance when you're tailing people, too. You were practically riding his bumper the whole way here."

"I was not," I protested.

"If you say so. I imagine the only reason he didn't notice you was because he was too busy ogling that young girl's breasts."

I was tempted to say they were, indeed, impressive, but that's not exactly something you want to admit to the woman you're dating.

Alana turned and looked at Dr. Peterson having sex with his date. She was still leaning against the balcony railing, but now her breasts were exposed and bouncing up and down. Apparently, Dr. Peterson had reached forward and pulled the top of her dress down while

Alana and I debated how bad a private investigator I was. I snapped another photo for Mrs. Peterson's collection.

"Could she have gotten bigger implants? Those things are huge," Alana said. "And don't think I didn't notice you take another photo."

"How do you know they're fake?" I asked. "And need I remind you, I'm here on official business."

"She's young and all, but nobody's natural boobs stand up like that," Alana said.

I scanned through the shots on the viewfinder.

"I think I've got more than enough to cook this guy."

We both watched them in action for a few more seconds.

"Man, he's really sticking it to her," I said.

"Don't be vulgar."

"Sorry."

"Still, it does create a certain stirring," she said.

"Are you suggesting what I think you're suggesting?"

"Only if you're game."

"I'm always game with you," I said.

"Your place or mine?" she asked.

"Yours. More privacy."

I followed Alana back to her house. It took us close to an hour because she lived near Ka'anapali. I was concerned she might have lost her desire after the long drive. I need not have worried. She was ready, willing, and more than able. We decided to re-create the Dr. Peterson scene on her patio. The backyard had large trees that surrounded the property and offered complete privacy.

I made two drinks in her kitchen and carried them outside. I found Alana sitting on one of her patio chairs.

"Care for a drink?" I asked.

"Why, yes, Dr. Peterson. I would like one," Alana said in her most bimbo-like voice.

I handed her the drink.

"I don't know what to call you," I admitted. "I never learned the young lady's name."

"Just call me Bambi."

I sat down beside Alana, and we sipped our drinks.

"That's strong," she said. "Are you trying to get me drunk, doctor?"

"How else am I going to convince someone as young and beautiful as you to sleep with an old guy like me?" I asked.

The truth was that at thirty years old, Alana was only five years younger than me.

"Your large wallet might help," she said.

I finished my drink and put it on the table.

"Have I told you how irresistible I find you, Bambi?"

"No, you haven't."

I leaned forward and kissed her.

"You are breathtaking," I said.

Within a few minutes, we had assumed the same position we last saw Dr. Peterson and his companion enjoying. The breeze was cool and it felt sensational running across our nude bodies. We both did our best to remain quiet. We didn't think her neighbors were outside, but you never know. There are a lot of Peeping Toms out there. Who knows who's hiding in the bushes?

2

THE FOUR C'S

THE NEXT MORNING I COPIED THE PHOTOS OF DR. PETERSON FROM MY camera to a jump drive and drove to Mara's office. She greeted me in the lobby. Mara is forty-five. She's tall with dark-red hair. Mara impressed me the moment I first met her. She's easily one of the most confident people I've ever met, but she doesn't exude an ounce of arrogance or smugness. She led me back to her office where she sat in a chair behind her desk. I sat across from her.

Mara plugged the drive into her laptop and scanned through the photos of Dr. Peterson and his young lover.

"Dear Lord," she said.

"Shocked me, too." I said.

"I never imagined you'd get something this good. Who's the girl?" Mara asked.

"No idea."

"I'm sure Karen will be delighted to see these. On the other hand, maybe not."

"Did you get the impression she's ready to divorce Peterson?" I asked.

"More than ready. You just made her millions."

I turned away from Mara.

"Something wrong?" she asked.

I turned back to her.

"I appreciate you giving me this job, but I've thought a lot about it and it's not something I can do anymore."

"Why not? You're clearly good at it."

"Photographing guys with their pants around their ankles is not something I imagined myself doing."

"That's what investigators do. They catch people doing things they aren't supposed to be doing."

"I was a paid Peeping Tom for God's sake."

"Better than being an unpaid Peeping Tom."

"You know what I mean," I said.

"So this means you're officially out?" she asked.

I nodded. "It's just not how I imagined it would be. I'm sorry."

"Don't worry about it. Perhaps something different will come along."

I stood and extended my hand. Mara stood as well and we shook hands.

"Thanks for taking a chance on me. Maybe we'll run into each other at the sushi place."

On a side note, I discovered during one of our earlier meetings that both Mara and I enjoy a sushi restaurant located near the airport, of all places. It has fantastic rainbow rolls.

"I'm sure we'll meet again. Take care, Mr. Rutherford."

I drove back to Foxx's house, where I currently rent a bedroom. Lauren left Foxx the house and the rights to her paintings in her will. It made him an instant millionaire many times over. The house is located on the coast in Ka'anapali. The back wall is basically one giant window that offers spectacular views of the ocean and sunset. There's a large pool in the backyard, and I usually swim several laps underwater after crawling out of bed each morning. I've lost count of how many hours I've spent just sitting by the pool and staring at the waves crashing onto the rock jetty just off the coastline beyond Foxx's backyard.

I found Foxx sitting by the pool when I got home. Foxx is a huge guy. He stands six-four and weighs around two-forty. He was a football player for the Washington Redskins before a bum knee forced his early retirement. Immediately after his last season, Foxx took a vacation to Maui, and he never returned home. He loved the sun, the casual lifestyle and, above all, the women. Foxx has a way with the fairer sex. He's usually with a new girl every other week, which made his close relationship with Lauren such a surprise. They were well on their way to marriage. Her death, a brutal one at that, devastated him. He's told me he's gotten over it, but I know him well enough to know he's not telling me the truth.

"How'd things go last night?" Foxx asked.

I filled him in on the details, including my visit with Mara Winters.

"Please tell me you kept copies of the photos," he said.

"Sorry, I deleted them."

"You inconsiderate bastard."

"Come on, Foxx. You wouldn't have respected me if I'd kept nude photos of that innocent young lady."

"You couldn't have at least given me one little peek before you erased them?"

I was spared having to answer when my dog darted out of the house and ran up to me. How much better would the world be if people greeted everyone else as enthusiastically as a dog does? Of course, it would be hilarious watching people get on their backs and roll around.

My dog's name is Maui; he was named after my new home, of course. He weighs just ten pounds, is black and silver in color, and is a cross between a Maltese and a Yorkshire terrier. He's more than a handful. I don't think I've ever encountered a more mischievous dog, but his cute face keeps me from giving him the boot. I bent over and rubbed his belly. I looked up at Foxx.

"What are you up to today?" I asked.

"I've got a lunch date with Suzy," Foxx said.

"Have I met her yet?"

"She was at the house a couple of nights ago."

"Brunette? I think I might have caught a glimpse of her. What's her story?"

"I met her at Harry's. She's an assistant manager for one of the hotels in Lahaina."

I didn't bother asking Foxx if he thought this relationship would last more than a few weeks. We both knew it wouldn't.

I told Foxx I'd catch him later and took Maui for a walk. Despite his short legs, Maui has no difficulty keeping up with me. This dog could walk for miles. Other than eating and sleeping, walking is definitely his favorite activity.

We walked for about an hour. Once we got back, Maui lay on the cool tiles of the living room floor, and I plopped down on the sofa with my laptop. I checked my email. I'm not exactly sure why since I rarely get any.

I then Googled engagement rings and immediately began to read about the four C's - cut, color, clarity, and carat weight. I saw the general rule of thumb is that you're supposed to spend three month's salary on a ring. I wasn't sure if that was gross salary or after taxes. I was jobless, however, so what did that mean for me? My parents were both wealthy and they left me a sizable inheritance. Technically, I didn't have to ever work another day in my life. I wasn't sure how I was supposed to factor that equation into the cost of the ring. It was all so confusing and intimidating, and I immediately logged off and closed the laptop.

A question then popped into my head. Why had I even searched for engagement rings? I didn't recall actually thinking about them and then making the decision to look for one on the Internet. It was sort of a subconscious thing, and the truth of the matter was that it thoroughly surprised me, even scared me a little. Alana and I hadn't been dating each other for that long, and we'd recently weathered a serious rough patch where I wasn't sure if we'd technically broken up or not. Was I seriously considering a marriage proposal to her, and if so, what did that mean?

I've never been married before. I haven't even considered it. It's not like I'm against marriage. I just haven't met anyone whom I remotely thought about being married to. Alana changed all of that, though. I knew that I loved her and that she loved me. I thought about her constantly, but how does one know when those feelings truly go beyond the initial stages of infatuation and transform into those deeper connections that are potentially lifelong? Were we technically past our honeymoon stage? How does one even know when that happens? I thought we were, especially considering the rough patch I mentioned a second ago. Did that mean my feelings for her were now more solid and less based on initial attraction and lust?

My cell phone rang. The display indicated the call was from Alana. What is that saying about ears burning?

"Hey, there," I said.

"Did you meet with Mara yet?"

"Yeah, I told her I wasn't interested in any more jobs like that."

"How do you feel about that? Do you think it's the right move?"

"Absolutely. I felt kind of gross watching them go at it."

"You shouldn't, but I understand what you're saying. Want to have dinner tonight?"

"Sure. Where do you want to go?"

"How about I come over? You can cook for Foxx and me."

"May I have the pleasure?"

"Yes, you may."

"What are you craving?" I asked.

"Nothing in particular. Surprise me. I better get back to work. See you tonight."

"See you."

I ended the call and debated what to make for dinner. I'm not a particularly good cook, so I have to keep my selections simple. My thoughts quickly drifted back to my conversation with Mara. It was true I didn't want to take on any more of those kinds of investigations, but I wasn't sure what I wanted to do instead. I knew I didn't want to live off the proceeds of my parents' hard work. It was a great problem to have. I knew I'd forever be grateful for the way they planned for my future. Nevertheless, we all want to forge our own paths and provide for ourselves. I thought about what I did enjoy, and only one thing popped into my mind – photography. I didn't want to ruin my passion for the craft by shooting weddings of demanding brides or photos of families all dressed in white shirts and khaki pants while posing on some scenic beach.

I'd been unemployed since the recession, which brought on the loss of my architecture job. As you can imagine, that profession took an enormous amount of education and training, only for me to realize it wasn't what I thought it was going to be. In fact, I had hated it.

In a strange way, I was grateful the recession took away the job. If it hadn't, I'd probably still be toiling away in my gray cubicle, completely dreading my day-to-day life. I certainly wouldn't have gotten around to visiting Foxx on Maui and eventually meeting Alana. Now I was left with a different question – what to do with the rest of my life.

The phone rang again, saving me from the dramatic ponderings on the meaning of life. I assumed it was Alana and that she had an idea of what she wanted to eat, but I didn't recognize the number on the display. I answered it anyway.

"Hello."

"Mr. Rutherford, it's Mara Winters."

I immediately wondered if she was going to try to tempt me with another Peeping Tom case.

"I have another job that I think you might be interested in," she said.

"It doesn't call for following unfaithful husbands, does it?"

"Nothing of the sort. It's potentially a much more serious subject. Any chance you can be back at my office in an hour? My client is coming over soon. I'm sorry for the late notice. This was just brought to my attention."

I hesitated a second, not sure if this was something I wanted to get into. Though I had thrown my problem out to the universe, and maybe this new assignment from Mara was the answer.

"Sure. I'll see you in an hour," I said.

"Great. See you soon."

I ended the call and looked down at Maui the dog. He was still sleeping on the tiled floor, but he had rolled over onto his back and his legs were sticking straight up in the air. This dog turned sleeping into an art form. I snapped a photo with my phone and texted it to Alana.

3

CHARLOTTE CHAMBERS

I drove to Mara's office and arrived before her client.

"Thanks for coming back here on such short notice," she said.

"No problem. So, what's this about?"

"I'm not quite sure. After you left, I received a call from a long-term client. She said it was a matter of life or death, but she wouldn't tell me exactly what it was about."

"Who is she?"

"Her name's Charlotte Chambers. She's the eighty-five-year-old owner of the Chambers Hotel in Wailea."

"Has she ever called you in a panic before?"

"Never. I urged her to call the police if someone was in danger, but she wouldn't hear of it."

I saw Mrs. Chambers drive into the parking lot a few minutes later. She arrived alone, and I was impressed she could get around by herself at her advanced age. Mrs. Chambers was tall and thin. Her posture was straight, and her walk was steady.

Mara introduced me to Mrs. Chambers and led us into her large office. We sat down on a sofa and chair that were placed several feet from her desk. It was somewhat of an informal area to talk as opposed to the typical desk with one or two chairs placed in front of it. I always found that arrangement to feel like an interrogation versus a conversation.

"Is everything all right, Mrs. Chambers?" Mara asked.

"It most certainly isn't. Someone tried to kill me last night," she responded.

"Did you call the police?" I asked.

"Absolutely not."

"Why wouldn't you call them if someone tried to harm you?" Mara asked.

"Because I don't want to get them involved. Next thing you know, the story will be all over the news, and people will mock the Chambers family."

"But if your life is in danger," Mara said.

"This needs to be handled another way," Mrs. Chambers said.

"Please tell us exactly what happened," I said.

"Every night, I take a hot bath before bed. Last night, someone tried to drown me."

"Did you see who it was?" I asked.

"No, they were too clever for that."

"I'm afraid I don't understand," Mara said.

"My wine was drugged. There's no other explanation."

"You were drinking wine in the tub?" Mara asked.

"I have two glasses of wine each night, one at dinner and one while I take my bath. Someone must have dropped something into the wine."

"Who would have been there to do that?" I asked.

"Patricia was the only one at the house yesterday other than me, but she usually leaves by five o'clock."

"Is there any way she could have drugged the wine before she left?" Mara asked.

"Of course, but she wouldn't have. Patricia and I are fine. She may be a little slow sometimes, but she's the best assistant I've had in years."

"Do you think you could have just fallen asleep?" I asked.

"I've taken a bath every night for decades. Never once have I ever fallen asleep or even almost fallen asleep in the tub."

She paused, and I really didn't know what else to say or ask at that point. I began to wonder if my earlier positive impression of her had been dead wrong. Perhaps she was off her rocker. It certainly seemed that way.

"I always keep a supply of wine in my pantry. It would be easy for someone to drug the wine earlier in the week. They could have injected the bottle with a needle through the cork. I've seen things like that on television," Mrs. Chambers said.

I glanced at Mara as subtly as I could. To her credit, she had a serious and concerned look on her face. I wasn't sure if she was faking it for her client's sake or if she was actually worried that her long-time client needed to be committed to a nursing home.

"What would you like us to do, Mrs. Chambers?" Mara asked.

"I want you to find out who did this to me."

Mara looked at me for suggestions. I turned to Mrs. Chambers.

"I don't suppose you still have the wine," I said.

"No, I poured the whole bottle down the drain. I know it was a foolish thing to do."

"You said you keep a supply in your pantry, though. Perhaps we can test another bottle. There was no way to guarantee which bottle you would have chosen last night. Maybe your attacker poisoned more than one."

Mrs. Chambers nodded. I felt bad for feeding into her fantasy, but I didn't know what else to do, short of wishing her a good day and immediately vacating the building.

"There's something else," she said. "I've received two letters in the mail in the last few weeks. They threatened my life."

"What did they say?" Mara asked.

"They said they were going to kill me. That my time was up."

"Did you keep them?" I asked.

"No, I was so upset that I threw them away."

"Were they typed or handwritten?" I asked.

"They were typed on white paper."

"Have you ever received any letters like that before?" I asked.

"Never," she said.

"Do you have any idea who might want to harm you?" Mara asked.

"I know exactly who did it." She paused. "One of my children."

"Your children?" I asked.

"The greedy bastards. One of them tried to off me."

I almost burst out laughing, but I managed to restrain myself.

"Why would they do that?" I asked.

"I was approached by a large company a few weeks ago. They offered to buy my hotel. They'd made the offer several times before, but this time the price they threw out was substantially more. You might even describe it as obscene. My children have pleaded with me to sell, but I won't do it."

"May I ask why?" I said.

"My late husband, Millard, made me swear on his deathbed that I would never sell the company. He built the hotel over fifty years ago, and it was an instant success. It's an older property now, but we still take good care of it. It makes a good amount of money for the family."

"I assume the land is what's so attractive to your potential buyer," Mara said.

"Yes, Millard was a genius when it came to business. He bought in an underdeveloped area and got some of the best real estate for next to nothing. Now the property is worth a fortune. My children want me to sell so they never have to work again. They're lazy, and they feel entitled. I'm convinced they want to see me gone so they can move forward with the deal."

"Did they threaten you? It's a big leap to go from wanting you to sell your land to trying to murder you in the bathtub," I said.

Plus the woman was eighty-five. I don't mean to sound insensitive, but for how much longer could the dear lady hang on? Why risk getting caught for murder when you can just wait a couple of years for her to naturally pass away? It wasn't like the land was going to lose value. On the other hand, drugging the wine was a brilliant way to get away with it. No one would have suspected foul play, and it was highly unlikely an autopsy would be performed. Did this mean I was now actually thinking she might have been the target of a nefarious plot? Not at all. These were just hypotheticals I ran through my mind as I sat in Mara's office.

"The family has had terrible fights in the last week. It's not just the offer to buy the hotel, though. My children can't stand each other. Each one thinks they're the only one in the family with any brains. They've all accused each other of almost ruining the company through incompetence."

"Is there any merit to these accusations?" I asked.

"Somewhat. They say certain characteristics skip a generation. None of my children possess the business acumen of my Millard."

"Forgive me if I'm giving you unwanted advice, Mrs. Chambers, but maybe it would be a good idea if you sold the hotel based on your lack of confidence in your children," I said.

"I just can't do that. It's the promise I made Millard. He's been gone over twenty years. I thought the pain would be less by now, but it isn't. I still miss him terribly. I can't break my promise to him."

I admired the woman's loyalty and commitment to her late husband.

"Mrs. Chambers, you said you wanted us to determine who drugged your wine. Does that mean you'd like us to open an investigation into this? Do you actually want us interviewing your children?" Mara asked.

"Yes, I need to find out who did this to me. I can't let that person inherit a portion of the estate. I won't allow it."

"Unfortunately, there's a distinct possibility we won't be able to discover who's responsible. What would you do then?" I asked.

"I don't even want to consider that possibility. You must determine who's guilty."

Mara turned to me.

"Is this something you can take on?" she asked.

Talk about putting me in the hot seat. I didn't want to take the case. I was still convinced she simply fell asleep in the tub. I hated the thought of letting Mrs. Chambers down, but I had no doubt that's exactly where this case would lead.

"Please take my case, Mr. Rutherford. I know they're going to try again. You have to figure out who's doing this to me."

"I really can't make any promises other than to do my best," I said.

"Thank you."

"What should be the first step?" Mara asked.

I had only conducted two previous investigations and still considered my solving those to be strokes of luck rather than professional skills. My technique, if you can even call it that, was fairly straightforward. It was mainly a matter of meeting with the likely suspects and looking for minor clues that pointed to inconsistencies and lies. Add enough of those lies together, search for a motive, and eventually the truth reveals itself.

"I'd like to meet with your family members," I said, "but I need to determine a way to speak with them without them realizing why I'm really there. I don't suppose you have any events coming up where they'll all be present, some sort of social gathering maybe."

"My husband's ninetieth birthday would have been in a few days. Perhaps I can throw him a birthday party of sorts. It would be a way to honor his memory."

"That's a fantastic idea. They won't be able to say no to that, and it will be a good chance for me to wander around and meet them all. Do me a favor, though. Invite plenty of friends and neighbors. Don't make it just a family gathering. My presence mustn't seem out of the ordinary."

"Is a few days enough time?" Mara asked.

"I have a good staff working for me. We can get anything done in that time."

"One more thing," I said. "Please make a list for me of your children and any pertinent information about each one. Photos of them would also be good."

Mrs. Chambers nodded. "Thank you again, Mr. Rutherford."

"What about the next few days? Do you want me to arrange for security?" Mara asked.

"No, Patricia will be there with me, and I won't be drinking any of the remaining wine."

Mara and I walked Mrs. Chambers to the door. After she drove off, Mara turned to me.

"Has she turned senile?" she asked.

"You would know better than me," I said. "This is my first time meeting her. I've seen no prior behavior to compare it to."

"Keep a record of your hours so we can bill her appropriately. This may be a waste of your time, so at least you'll get paid for it."

After leaving Mara's office, I drove to the grocery store to buy ingredients for dinner with Alana and Foxx. One of the few downsides to living on Maui is the high cost of groceries because most things have to be shipped from the mainland. After much thought and consideration, I decided to make chili which I realize is by no means a classic Hawaiian dish, but it's one of the few items I actually know how to make. My talents don't go much beyond chopping vegetables and boiling water.

Once I got home, I took Maui the dog for another long walk and then cooled down by swimming underwater laps in the pool. Foxx was nowhere to be found, and I assumed he was gallivanting around with his new gal, Suzy. I admired Foxx's natural ability with women. I used to be jealous of it. That's not easy to admit, but it's the truth. My relationship with Alana is probably the only reason I'm not jealous anymore. We're very comfortable around each other. I wouldn't want to replace that with the excitement of meeting someone new. Foxx, on the other hand, loves the experience of getting to know someone. I knew Suzy would most likely not last. I didn't feel sorry for her because I figured she probably already knew it, too, and was apparently okay with it. I realize that women are way smarter than men in probably every category, so I had no doubt Suzy knew what the deal was.

I took a shower and then headed into the kitchen to lay out the various ingredients for dinner. Foxx arrived a few minutes later. He was alone.

"Where's Suzy?" I asked. "I thought you said she was going to be with you."

"I'm pretty sure Suzy and I are no longer seeing each other."

"That fast?" I looked at my watch. "By my calculations, you still had another week or so before you got tired of her."

"Yeah, but she accused me of flirting with another woman."

"Were you?"

"You know me. I flirt with everyone."

The doorbell rang, and Maui the dog took off running toward the front door.

"I'll get it," Foxx said.

Foxx followed Maui to the door and a second later I heard two female voices. I immediately recognized Alana's telling Foxx hello. I wondered if Suzy had a change of heart and was the other person with Alana, but then I recognized the voice.

"Look who Alana brought with her," Foxx said.

I turned around from the kitchen counter and saw Alana's sister, Hani, standing beside her. For those of you who didn't read my last tale, Hani is Alana's younger sister. She's equally stunning, although I would never admit that to Alana. I wasn't even aware of Hani's existence until a few months ago. She grew up on Maui but spent the last year in Los Angeles pursuing a modeling career. She recently moved back to the island and, like Foxx and me, was currently trying to figure out what to do with herself. I wouldn't call Hani a dishonest person, but she has a way of withholding vital information. This trait, and a few other things I won't go into, was the reason Alana and Hani had a terrible relationship. For all practical purposes, they weren't even talking to each other until a recent legal matter and the death of a loved one brought them closer together. I wasn't sure how long this was going to last, but I certainly hoped it would be permanent. Like all high emotions where family is involved, you just never know.

"When I told Hani you were making chili, she asked if she could come along," Alana said.

"The more the merrier," I said.

"Make it spicy, please," Hani said.

I unwrapped the ground meat from the plastic package and walked over to the stove. I turned it on medium and placed a pan on it.

"Foxx and I were just talking about his flirting," I said.

"Oh, great," Foxx groaned.

"What about his flirting?" Alana asked.

"His new girl, Suzy, just broke things off because she thought he was flirting with another woman," I said.

"Can't anything be private around here?" Foxx asked.

"Were you flirting?" Hani asked.

"We were at Harry's getting a drink, and I struck up a conversation with a woman at the bar," Foxx admitted.

"You did this right in front of Suzy?" Alana asked.

"Not exactly. She was in the bathroom at the time."

"So you waited until she went to the bathroom to hit on the other woman?" Hani asked.

"Who said I was hitting on her? I was just talking to her."

"At least, that's what he told Suzy when she walked out. My guess is she saw you pass the woman your phone number," I said.

Foxx said nothing.

"Oh my God, I'm right, aren't I?" I asked.

"Listen. It's not like Suzy and I were exclusive. We didn't even have that conversation," Foxx said.

I laughed and started chopping the vegetables.

"Do you need any help?" Alana asked me.

"No, I'm great. Just grab some beers for you and Hani. I just stocked the fridge."

Alana walked over to the refrigerator and pulled out two beers. She handed one to Hani.

"Thanks," Hani said.

"You want one, Foxx?" Alana asked.

"Sure. It looks like I may need a few."

Alana pulled a couple more beers out and handed them to Foxx. He immediately popped the top off one and took a long gulp.

"What's the deal, Foxx? You can't commit to a woman?" Hani asked.

Alana gave me a quick look. We both knew Hani didn't know the details of Lauren's death, and she had no way of knowing how much Foxx cared for her. To his credit, Foxx let the comment roll off. He took another long pull from his beer.

"There aren't that many women worth committing to," Foxx said. "Present company excluded, of course."

"Of course," Alana said.

I dropped the meat onto the hot pan and stirred it around.

"Don't be too hard on him, ladies. He's always been this way. It's a birth defect," I said.

Foxx laughed.

"I wouldn't call it that. It's just that half of all marriages end in divorce. Why put yourself through that?"

I instantly thought back to my morning Internet search for engagement rings. Was I making a mistake to even consider proposing to Alana? I wondered if that marriage statistic was even correct. I'd heard it many times before, and it's been said so often that people now took it as gospel. I had no way of knowing if it was actually true, and even if it were, how many of those divorces were from repeat offenders? I had a few former co-workers at the architecture firm who had each been divorced three times.

"I think the idea of marriage is a very romantic thing," Hani said.

"Oh God, I'm sorry, Hani. I wasn't even thinking," Foxx said.

When Foxx and I first met Hani, she'd just announced her marriage plans. It didn't work out for her.

"It's okay," she said.

"No, it's not. I feel like a giant ass," Foxx said. "I'm always sticking my foot in my mouth."

Hani laughed.

I wasn't sure how to respond.

"Let's change the subject," Alana said. She turned to me. "Why don't you tell Hani about your first professional investigation?"

I groaned.

"Please, let's try to avoid that subject."

"Now you have to tell me," Hani said.

I reluctantly told Hani about following Doctor Peterson and photographing his extramarital activities on the balcony of his beach house.

"He actually went for it right there in the open?" Hani asked.

"Technically, he wasn't exactly out in the open. There was some privacy," I said.

"Except for you and Alana hiding in the bushes," Hani said.

"There's that, yes," I said.

I put the browned meat and the chopped vegetables into a large pot.

"What happened when you went back to see Mara? Did she give you a new case?" Alana asked.

I filled them in on my conversation with Mara and Mrs. Chambers.

"That poor woman. I can't believe one of her kids would try to murder her," Hani said.

"You don't think that actually happened, do you?" Alana asked me.

"Not at all, but I couldn't say no to the lady. I really felt bad for her."

"So she's going through with the party?" Foxx asked.

"As far as I know, which is one of the things I wanted to bring up tonight. Is there any chance you guys can come to the party with me? There are a lot of members of the Chambers family, and I'll need help talking to all of them."

"Divide and conquer?" Alana asked.

"Something like that," I said.

"You actually expect to uncover some big murder scheme?" Foxx asked.

"Not a chance. I just want to give this lady some peace of mind. There's no reason for her to spend her last years being paranoid."

"At the very least, we get a free party out of it," Foxx said.

"Count me in," Alana said.

Hani turned to Foxx.

"Does that make you and me dates for the party?" she asked.

"Sure. Just don't get mad at me if you see me talking to some other woman."

I finished preparing the chili and turned the stove to a low setting.

"Well, it's going to be about an hour before this is ready," I said.

"Why don't we go out to the pool," Alana suggested.

I grabbed a few more beers from the refrigerator and we all walked outside. The sun was setting and the colors were beautiful.

"You've got a hell of a view, Foxx," Alana said.

"It's extraordinary. I never take it for granted," he said.

Alana, Foxx, and I sat in wooden chairs, while Hani sat on the side of the pool and dipped her legs into the water.

"The water's so warm," she said.

Maui the dog ran up to her, which somewhat surprised me considering he'd never taken to her before. Hani smiled and scratched him on the top of his head. Hani turned to me.

"Have you and Foxx always been friends?" she asked.

"I can't really remember a time when we weren't," I said.

"If you knew this guy the way I know him, you'd be shocked at how well things have turned out for him," Foxx said.

"Oh, you have to tell me more," Alana said.

"Poe was always the skinniest kid on the block. I was constantly protecting him from the bullies. What did you weigh in high school? A buck-fifty?"

"If that," I admitted.

"That's pretty thin for someone of your height," Alana said.

I nodded. "I couldn't gain weight. At the time, I didn't appreciate what a nice problem that was to have."

"And now he's living on Maui and dating a hot lady like Alana. Man, you should have seen how bad he was with the women before."

Alana and Hani laughed.

"How did this turn into Poe's most embarrassing moments?" I asked.

"Do you remember that girl you went to the prom with? What was her name?" Foxx asked.

"I tried to block it," I said.

"Tina or Tara?"

"Tonya, I think, or maybe it was Tina," I admitted.

"It took weeks for Poe to summon up the courage to ask her out."

"Why? Was she super pretty?" Alana asked.

"She was nice looking, but Poe was too terrified to ask anyone out."

"Thanks, Foxx," I said.

"Poe finally asks her out and she says yes. Then she spends the entire prom dancing with this other guy."

"She didn't dance with you at all?" Alana asked me.

"One or two dances, but she seemed to do everything she could to avoid me," I said.

"That's horrible," Hani said.

"Turned out she really wanted to go to the prom with this other guy, but her parents wouldn't allow it," Foxx said.

"That's about the saddest thing I've ever heard," Alana said.

"They actually got married sometime after school, so at the very least, I like to think I had a small part to play in their relationship succeeding," I said.

"Poor baby," Alana said.

"Oh, I forgot to tell you I saw on Facebook they got a divorce," Foxx said.

"She probably couldn't stop pining for me after all these years. The memory of me drove the poor woman to leave her husband. I just hope she doesn't turn up on our doorstep."

I took a swig of my beer. We told more stories designed to humiliate me. I didn't mind. I knew it was all in good fun, and I was able to get in plenty of embarrassing stories about Foxx, too.

Eventually, the chili was ready. We filled up our bowls and ate outside to enjoy the pleasant night air. The food wasn't bad, but everyone was kind enough to tell me how tasty it was. Hani did mention it could have been spicier.

We went inside after finishing dinner. Foxx turned on the television while I washed the dishes. He flipped over to the Discovery Channel. The guy has a thing for shows about couples killing each other. I really don't have any clue how that has anything to do with "discovery." I thought that channel used to be about science. Of course, I could be wrong about that.

As it turned out, Hani was also a big fan of those shows, but who am I to judge? I kept my mouth shut, which is rather hard for me to do. Instead, I concentrated on finishing the dishes. I heard the dog whine and looked down at him. He was sitting at my feet and looking up at me.

"Is he hungry?" Alana asked.

"Always, but in this case, I think he has to use the bathroom."

"Want to walk him?" she asked.

I grabbed Maui's leash, and Alana and I left Foxx and Hani watching television. They both seemed utterly absorbed in watching the murder unfold on TV.

"You'd think if anyone wouldn't like that stuff, it would be those two," Alana said after we got outside.

"Human beings. You can never figure them out."

"I hope Foxx didn't embarrass you earlier tonight."

"Not at all."

"Sorry your teenage years were so rough."

"Isn't everybody's?" I asked.

"About this party, how can we make this assignment fun?"

"I was just thinking about that. Maybe we should take on new identities. I can be a timeshare salesman here at a convention, and you can be my escort for the night."

"Very funny. I might have actually gone through with it if we weren't living on an island and most likely going to run into some of these people again."

"Have you ever met any member of the Chambers family?" I asked.

"I don't think so. I went to a wedding reception years ago that was held at their hotel, but I don't know if I met anyone from the family."

"The mother described her adult children as lazy and entitled," I said.

"Should make for a pleasant evening."

As Alana and I continued to walk the dog, I thought about Mara's last words to me right before I left her office. "You may be wasting your time, so at least you'll get paid for it." I don't want to get all depressed on you since I know you're reading this story for entertainment, but how many of us have jobs where we feel like we constantly waste our time only so we can get paid? I definitely didn't want to be falling into another trap like I had with the architecture job.

I would go to the party as a favor to Mrs. Chambers, but if I didn't come up with anything substantial during the event, I would inform Mara that I was no longer able to pursue the case. At the time, I assumed that meant I would be finished with the case in a couple of days. I had no way of knowing just how wrong I was.

4

THE PARTY

I RECEIVED A PACKAGE FROM MARA'S OFFICE THE MORNING OF THE party. It contained copies of photographs of Charlotte Chambers' adult children and a brief description of them, all written by her, I presumed.

Millard Chambers Jr., sixty years old, and his wife, Jen, also sixty. "Mill" is the oldest child. Mill and Jen met in college. Jen hasn't worked a day in her life. Mill and Jen have twin boys, both of whom graduated from Stanford University. They both live in San Francisco and work for technology companies. Mill feels the company should be handed over to him because he's the oldest, has worked for the company the longest, and is already the general manager.

Bethany, fifty-six years old, and her husband, Barry Williams, fifty-seven years old. Bethany is the middle child. She can't stand her two brothers and has always believed they were favored over her because she's a woman. She and Barry have one child, a girl named Olivia. Olivia graduated from the University of Southern California and spent several years in Los Angeles working in the entertainment industry. Olivia recently moved back to Maui and started a wedding planning company.

Joe Chambers, fifty years old. He has had substance abuse problems but has been clean for over two years. He is unmarried and has no children.

Nothing jumped out at me or seemed out of the ordinary beyond her obvious dislike of her daughter-in-law and the fact her son-in-law shares a name with one of the Brady Bunch actors. I flipped through the photos again and made superficial observations. Mill and Jen's photograph must have been taken at a funeral, either that, or they're two of the most miserable looking people I've ever seen. I didn't know what Charlotte's deceased husband looked like, but I guessed Mill took after him because I didn't see any resemblance between Mill and Charlotte. It was difficult to determine their height. They were both of average weight.

Bethany and Barry looked much happier. They were both quite large. Bethany's facial features reminded me a lot of Charlotte.

Joe Chambers got all of the looks in the family. He was a handsome guy with an insanely full head of hair for someone his age. His photo was taken on a beach. He was shirtless. The guy was in good shape, I'll give him that.

I shoved the photos and Charlotte's notes back into the envelope. I called Alana and told her that Foxx and I would pick Hani and her up around six thirty. I had expected Charlotte would throw an afternoon event because of her age. I doubted an eighty-five-year-old would want to party into the evening, but the invitation stated the event would start at seven.

We took Foxx's Lexus SUV since my two-seater was way too small. Alana opened the front door to her house just as Foxx and I pulled into the driveway. She and Hani both wore white shorts that showed off their firm, tanned legs. Alana wore a white, loose top with long sleeves. Hani had on a dark-blue tank top.

"Those girls are gorgeous," Foxx said.

"Don't get any ideas," I said. "I'd advise you to stay clear of Hani. She's dangerous."

"I've got news for you, Poe. They're all dangerous."

Alana and Hani hopped in the back seat.

"Hey, you two," Alana said.

"Thanks for doing this for me," I said.

"No problem. Everyone loves a party," Hani said.

I handed Alana the package I got from Mara.

"Here's a description of each person we're scoping out tonight."

Alana opened the package and removed the photos. The top photo was of Mill and Jen. Hani burst out laughing and then covered her mouth.

"You okay?" Foxx asked.

"Sorry. They just look so..."

"Miserable." Alana finished her sentence.

"The basic rundown is they all want their mother to sell to this giant hotel company. She refuses to sell, and they're pissed about it," I said.

"Which hotel company?" Alana asked.

"I don't know. She just said it was an obscene offer for the property, and none of them would ever have to work another day in their lives." I then told them about Charlotte's promise to her late husband that she'd never sell the company.

"Things change, though. I think she should sell, especially if all the kids hate each other. Seems like she's inadvertently setting her family up for failure," Foxx said.

"I agree, but it's her decision," I said.

It was a long drive to Mrs. Chambers' house. It turned out she lived right down the street from Doctor Peterson's beach house in Wailea. Mrs. Chambers' property is three times as large as his, though. It's a beautiful, multilevel house that reminded me of something Frank Lloyd Wright would have designed. We saw a valet as we approached the house.

"Classy," Foxx said.

Foxx stopped alongside the valet, and we all got out of the SUV. We made our way inside and saw dozens of people milling about. The home was even more impressive inside. There were glass walls everywhere that showcased the tremendous views along the coast. *Wow* was the word that immediately came to my mind. The other word was *expensive*. I don't mean to imply that Mara downplayed the family's wealth, but it didn't seem like they would ever be hurting even if they closed their hotel today. If the larger hotel company's offer was enough to impress the Chambers' kids, it must have been something else. I'm guessing lots and lots of zeroes were at the end.

"So, where do we start?" Alana asked.

"I'm going to find the bar," Foxx said.

"I'll join you," Hani said.

Foxx and Hani turned one way, and Alana and I went in the opposite direction. We walked into the living room and saw Mara talking with Mrs. Chambers.

"Mara, Mrs. Chambers," I said as we approached them.

Mara nodded to Alana and me.

"I'm so glad you could make it, Mr. Rutherford," Mrs. Chambers said.

"Mrs. Chambers, I'd like to introduce you to my girlfriend, Alana Hu."

"It's a pleasure to meet you," Alana said, and she extended her hand.

"Likewise," Mrs. Chambers said.

They shook hands. Alana looked around the room.

"You have a lovely home," she said.

"Thank you. My Millard designed it."

"I didn't know your husband was an architect, too," I said.

"Oh, he wasn't. He just sketched out what he wanted, and then we hired an architect to make sure it would work. I remember the day like it was just last week. We were eating lunch at a restaurant in Lahaina, and Millard took a napkin and drew the plans. He had to borrow a pen from the waitress. Ninety-five percent of this place is exactly as he envisioned it that day. I still have the sketch somewhere in the attic."

"He sounds like he was a very talented man," Mara said.

"He was. My Millard could do anything he set his mind to."

A waiter walked by with a tray and offered champagne to Alana and me. I took two glasses for us.

"You said today Mr. Chambers would have been ninety. Is that correct?" I asked.

"That's right."

"I'd like to propose a toast then to your late husband. To the man he was and the wonderful memories he evokes," I said.

We all raised our glasses.

"To my Millard."

We sipped our champagne. I found it to be quite good, which surprised me because I usually don't like the taste.

"Well, Mrs. Chambers, I'd better get to work," I said.

"Thank you again, Mr. Rutherford," she said.

"Do you have a moment?" Mara asked me.

"Of course."

Mara, Alana, and I left Mrs. Chambers and walked toward the corner of the living room.

"I spoke with Charlotte before the party. She's gotten a lot worse since our meeting. She's completely terrified someone is trying to kill her," Mara said.

"You believe her now?" Alana asked.

"No, I just don't know how to help the poor woman. I certainly can't go to her family. I offered again to take her to the police, but she still refuses."

"Unfortunately, I don't think there's anything the police could do," Alana said. "A woman in her eighties who falls asleep while drinking wine and taking a hot bath...no one would ever suspect foul play."

"She did get two threatening letters," Mara said.

"Yes, but Poe told me she threw them away."

"So what do we do?" Mara asked.

"How about this," I said, "I'll write up a lengthy report for her after the party and let her know I don't suspect anything. We'll even offer to have the remaining wine bottles tested."

"I can give you the name of the lab we use," Alana said.

"Hopefully that will make her feel better, and with time, she should eventually just let it drop," I said.

"I hope it works. Thanks again for doing this. On a lighter note, maybe I shouldn't put it that way, but I heard back from Karen Peterson this afternoon. Your photos sunk the doctor. He's begging her to take him back, but Karen has already started the divorce proceedings."

"I hope the other woman was worth it," Alana said.

Worth millions? I asked myself. I didn't think so, and I felt a little guilty for the part I played in Peterson's downfall. It was true I didn't force the guy to cheat, but we're all far from perfect.

Alana and I told Mara we'd talk to her later in the evening. We searched for Mrs. Chambers' adult children throughout the house. We didn't find them, so we decided to go outside. We immediately saw a huge seashell-shaped swimming pool that dominated the backyard. There was a large patio circling it. We spotted Bethany and Barry Williams a few seconds later. They were munching on hors d'oeuvres on the opposite side of the pool. They were only a few feet away from a large table that was covered in snacks. Bethany inherited her mother's height, but she was round versus thin. Barry was the same height as her and he was equally plump.

"How do we introduce ourselves?" Alana asked.

"I still can't convince you to do the timeshare salesman-escort thing?" I asked.

"Be serious, Poe."

"Okay, I say we just casually walk up to them and say hello. It's a party. That's what people do."

The couple turned and headed for the food table as we approached, so we followed them over there.

"It all looks delicious," I said.

"Difficult to tell what to get," Alana said.

"It is delicious, isn't it?" Bethany said.

We introduced ourselves to the couple and after a few minutes of small talk, Bethany asked us how we knew her mother.

"We're friends with your mother's attorney, Mara Winters. We ran into her, and she told us about the party. She said your mother told her to bring along some friends, so here we are."

"Your mother mentioned this party was to celebrate what would have been your father's ninetieth birthday," Alana said.

"He was a wonderful man. We all miss him so much," Bethany said.

"I'm sure," I said.

"Do you know how he passed? He was playing golf with some friends and dropped to the ground after hitting a great shot. He died of a stroke right there on the fifteenth fairway." Barry laughed.

"Not a bad way to go," I said.

"The man could do anything. He was a brilliant businessman and great golfer. He even designed this house," Bethany said, and she pointed to the house as if I didn't know where it was.

"Your mother mentioned that when we spoke inside," I said.

"Mara said your mother still runs the family business. Is that right?" Alana asked.

I was grateful to Alana for bringing the business up in such a subtle way. It was a wonderful move, and I studied Bethany and Barry for reactions. I wasn't disappointed. Their levity instantly vanished.

"I can't tell you how many times I've told my mother she should retire. She simply doesn't need the stress," Bethany said.

"So she really does still run the company? I thought Mara was joking," I said.

"I wish she was. Barry and I make most of the day-to-day decisions, but mother still likes to be involved."

"You and Barry manage the hotel then?" I asked.

"That's right," Bethany said.

That didn't really make a lot of sense to me. I wasn't sure how they could make the major decisions if her mother still technically ran the company. Also, Mrs. Chambers specifically mentioned in her notes that her oldest child Mill was the general manager. Maybe they were just trying to look like big shots in front of Alana and me, but the simple fact was they had just lied to us. A small lie? Sure. But maybe it was indicative of their characters. We spoke for several more minutes about the challenges of being in the hotel business. I wish I could say I found the conversation stimulating, but the truth was it was difficult to not fall asleep even though I was standing. If I heard one more comment about the new software they got to handle reservations, I might have dived fully clothed into the swimming pool just to escape.

The only interesting observation I made during the conversation was that both Bethany and Barry were simply too dull to have thought up a plan to secretly poison Mrs. Chambers. Granted, I never thought for a second that any of the children were guilty, but it helped to make the evening more fun if I allowed myself to believe there was a slim chance this murderous plot was actually true. I just didn't see them as having the imagination to cook up such an idea. They could have easily just have bored her to death with talk of the hotel, though. Mrs. Chambers was also in the business and would have found the topic far more interesting than I did, but Bethany and Barry had a way of talking that I suspected would have rendered any topic dull. They didn't talk so much as drone on and on.

I looked over to Alana and almost laughed when I saw the smile plastered on her face. I knew what she was doing. She forced this fake smile so she wouldn't appear as bored as me, but the smile was so huge I knew it wasn't genuine. If she wasn't so darn good looking, she might have come across like Jack Nicholson as the Joker. Fortunately, Bethany and Barry were so engaged in talking about themselves that I suspect they didn't notice both Alana and I were close to committing hara-kiri. Scratch Bethany and Barry Williams off my imaginary suspect list.

Alana and I eventually drifted away from the couple when they headed back to the table for more snacks. We left the pool area and went searching for Bethany's siblings. We ran into Foxx and Hani first. They were in the kitchen, enjoying what looked like a dirty martini and a whiskey sour.

"How's it going, guys?" I asked.

Foxx turned to me.

"I know what you're thinking. Hani and I have been doing nothing but taking advantage of the free drinks," Foxx said.

"I wasn't thinking that at all, but now that you've mentioned it..."

"We actually have something to report," Hani said.

"Lay it on us," Alana said. "It's bound to be more interesting than what we just lived through." Alana turned to me. "You owe me big for this."

Hani looked around the kitchen to see if there was anyone else within earshot. There wasn't.

"You know the youngest son who supposedly has been clean for a couple of years?" Hani whispered.

"I think his name's Joe," I said.

"Well, he's off the wagon," Hani said.

"You saw him drinking?" Alana asked.

"Better," Hani said, and she turned to Foxx. "You tell them."

Foxx hesitated. I knew he didn't like spying on people. I couldn't blame him.

"Out with it, Foxx," Alana said.

"I went into the bathroom and found him doing a line of coke on the counter."

"Here? In the house?" I asked.

"I guess he thought the door was locked. The dude freaked out when he saw me. I told him not to worry about it, and I left."

"Did he say anything after he came out?" Alana asked.

"Nope. He walked right past me and Hani and didn't even make eye contact. I haven't seen him since."

That's interesting, I thought, but I had no desire to add more stress and pressure to Mrs. Chambers by putting it in my report.

"What about you guys? Any luck?" Hani asked.

We filled Foxx and Hani in on our conversation by the pool.

"That does sound like an awesome software system for reservations," Foxx said. "I'm sorry I missed that conversation."

"I'm pretty sure I'm now an expert on it. I may teach a class," I said.

"That just leaves Mill and Jen," Hani said.

"We saved the best for last," I said.

Alana and I left the kitchen and went back on the hunt. We eventually found them near the beach. They were talking to another couple. We waited at a discreet distance and then moved in once the other couple left.

"Can you believe this view?" I said.

Mill and Jen turned to us.

"It was a hell of a place to grow up," Mill said.

We introduced ourselves to Mill and Jen and, of course, discovered what we already knew. Mill was the oldest son of Charlotte and Millard Chambers. He grew up on Maui and now ran their hotel. I didn't bother mentioning that his sister told us she basically ran the company. I also didn't mention that Mill's mother thought it important to write in her notes that Jen supposedly never worked a day in her life.

"You're the first Millard I've ever met," I said.

"It was a tough name to grow up with," he admitted.

"Well, I see your Millard and raise you an Edgar Allan," I said.

"Ah, that's why people call you Poe."

"I can relate is my point," I said.

"Yes, I'm sure you can. Fortunately, we both found beautiful women who were willing to overlook our unfortunate names."

I thought the comment a smooth move on Mill's part, but putting Jen in the same company as Alana was like comparing a child's paint-by-numbers kit with a masterpiece like the Mona Lisa. Regardless of the truth of Mill's statement, Jen squeezed his hand, and I knew he had accomplished his intention. Alana thanked him for the compliment as well.

We spoke for several minutes. Mill described what it was like growing up on Maui. We asked him about his father and, like his siblings, he had nothing but glowing things to say about Millard Sr.

Alana asked how Mill and Jen met. They confirmed they met in college. Mill described how he first spotted Jen as she sat under a tree reading one of her text books. He was so sappy about the encounter it sounded like he was reciting a romance novel by a second-rate writer, but I could tell Jen loved every minute of it. They asked us how we met, and Alana told the story of me stepping on her toes at an art show. It was a true story, unfortunately, and I was glad she left out the part about the murder investigation that essentially started within minutes of me accidentally stomping on her delicate toes. I really wished she had stuck to my fantasy story in which I was a timeshare salesman.

All together it was a pleasant conversation, and my instincts told me this couple could not have planned the demise of Mrs. Chambers either. It did raise an interesting question, though. If everyone was so nice, why was Mrs. Chambers utterly convinced one of her children was wicked enough to kill her? Obviously there were dark secrets under the surface waiting to be uncovered. On the other hand, maybe Mrs. Chambers was just losing it. Maybe the stress of running a company was enough to cause her to invent dastardly deeds when there were none present. There was also the pressure of the potential sale of their company. That had to weigh heavily on her.

We spoke with the couple for a few more minutes when Mara approached us.

"I need to borrow you two," she said.

I could instantly tell by the look on her face that something was wrong. She spoke in a hushed tone as we walked back toward the house.

"I told Mrs. Chambers about your plan to have the remaining wine bottles tested. She told me she would pull out a few bottles for you. A minute ago, she showed me a note she found in the pantry when she went to get the wine," Mara said.

"What did it say?" Alana asked.

"I think it's better for you to read it for yourselves. She's in her bedroom now. She still has the note."

We increased our pace and made our way to her bedroom which was on the second floor of the house. It was a massive master bedroom, which overlooked the pool and the ocean, but I didn't have much time to take in any other details because I saw the look of fear on Mrs. Chambers' face as she sat on the side of her bed. The note was clutched in her hand. I turned to Alana.

"Mrs. Chambers, may we see the note?" Alana asked.

Mrs. Chambers didn't say anything. She just held out the note. Alana carefully took it by the edges. She held the paper up so we could both read it. It was black type on plain white paper. I'm not an expert on font styles by any means, but it looked like your typical Times New Roman. The note read: "You know how this ends."

Alana and I looked at each other. We were both at a complete loss for words.

"What do we do?" Mara asked.

"I'm not leaving my home. I'm not letting this person scare me away," Mrs. Chambers said.

Too late for that, I thought. I didn't blame her for being scared, but I had a hard time believing the threat could have come from one of her children. The two couples seemed like decent people. I thought about the youngest child, Joe. Foxx had seen him doing drugs at the party in his mother's house, of all places. Of course, that didn't mean he wrote the note.

"Mrs. Chambers, Alana is a police detective," I said. Before I could continue, she snapped at me.

"I thought I said I didn't want the police involved."

"I didn't invite her here as a detective. She's my girlfriend, but now that we've seen this note, I think you need to get her officially involved."

"You need protection, Mrs. Chambers. I can arrange for a security company to protect you. We can also launch an investigation into these threats," Alana said.

"I don't know. I just don't know."

Mrs. Chambers was a very proud woman. I understood her fears of having her family problems dragged into the public arena, but I couldn't allow the woman to keep her life in jeopardy.

"I insist, Mrs. Chambers. You hired me to discover who made this attack against you. If you want me to stay on, the security company is part of the deal."

Mrs. Chambers hesitated and then nodded. I turned to Alana.

"How soon can you get someone here?" I asked.

"Tomorrow morning, probably."

"This is a big house, Mrs. Chambers. I'm sure you have a spare bedroom for me. I'd like to spend the night here until the security company can take over," I said.

Mrs. Chambers hesitated again, and I feared I would not be able to convince her to let me stay. I was about to plead my case again when she spoke.

"Very well. There's a spare room down the hall," she said.

"I'll go make some calls. I'll be back in a few minutes," Alana said, and she left the room.

"Mara said you found the note in the pantry. Is that correct?" I asked.

"Yes. It was slid between two bottles. I pulled one of the bottles out for you to test, and the note floated to the floor."

"And you still think it's one of your children?" I asked.

"I can't think of anyone else. They're really the only people I interact with."

"Did any of them confront you tonight?"

"No. They all expressed how much they missed their father and told me what a wonderful idea this party was."

I told her they had made the same comments to me. Alana returned and told us she'd arranged for a security company to be here first thing in the morning. She pressed for tonight, but they couldn't arrange it in such short order. They planned to send two guards. One would walk the surroundings, and the other would be posted inside the house.

"Alana and I can't stay without raising suspicion, especially if you think one of your children is responsible. Didn't you tell Mara and I that you had a personal assistant?" I asked.

"Yes, she's here somewhere. I told Patricia to enjoy the party and not worry about working tonight."

"Please call her and ask her to stay with you in this room. Once everyone has left, she should call me. Alana and I won't be far away. We'll be back at the house in no time and stand watch until the security firm arrives in the morning."

Mrs. Chambers reached for her phone on the nightstand. Alana and I headed downstairs while Mara waited in the bedroom for Patricia to arrive. The party was in full swing, and I guessed it would be hours before everyone left. Bethany and Barry departed early in the evening. I caught a glimpse of them as they headed to the door. They looked tired. I never did see Mrs. Chambers' youngest child, Joe, although I did search for him thoroughly. Alana and I stayed at the party until almost everyone had left. It was us, another couple I didn't know, and Mill and Jen. We said goodbye to them and exited the front door. Foxx and Hani were waiting for us outside.

"What do you want us to do? I don't mind staying with you guys," Foxx said.

"Can you take Hani home and then come back for us in the morning?" I asked.

"Sure. No problem."

We said goodbye and then Alana and I walked down the street past a few houses and cut over to the beach. We sat on the sand and looked out at the water. The moon was full and it cast a soft white light across the ocean.

"I find it so weird when these bad things happen in such a beautiful place," I said.

Alana said nothing, but I knew she was asking herself the same question. How could someone threaten an elderly woman like Charlotte Chambers?

We sat on the beach for about thirty minutes. Neither of us had anything more to say. My cell phone vibrated. It was Mrs. Chambers' assistant, Patricia. She told me everyone had left, including Mara. We stood and headed down the beach until we arrived at the house.

We walked through the yard to the front of the house so as not to frighten Patricia by knocking on the backdoor.

"Is she any better?" Alana asked as Patricia opened the door.

"She's asleep now. The stress has worn her out," Patricia said.

Not to mention the time, I thought. It was after two in the morning. I was exhausted myself. I'm sure Alana was as well.

We entered the house and followed Patricia to the living room.

"I have a room down the hall from her. I'll spend the night too," Patricia said.

"Thank you for your help," I said.

"Of course. Mrs. Chambers means so much to me."

Patricia headed upstairs while Alana and I elected to remain in the living room. We didn't turn the television on because we were worried we would disturb Mrs. Chambers. Instead, we sat on the sofa and spoke quietly.

"I doubt anyone will make a move tonight. They'd probably come at the house from the beachside, and anyone can easily see us in this house through all these windows," Alana said.

"Do you think that note is just meant to scare her?" I asked.

"Probably. At least now we have concrete proof that something is really going on. I feel bad about this, but I really thought she was making the whole thing up for attention."

"I can send those bottles out tomorrow," I said. I looked at my watch. It was close to three. "Or today, I should say."

Alana and I sat in silence a few more minutes. The sofa was incredibly comfortable, and it was difficult not to fall asleep. Alana leaned forward and picked up a photo book that was on the table in front of the sofa. The title was "The Chambers Family Travels." Alana scanned the book. There were several shots of the family in well-known tourist spots throughout Europe, Asia, and Africa.

"This family gets around," Alana said.

She continued to flip through the book.

"I've been to several of those locations," I said.

"I didn't know you traveled that much."

"It was with my parents, really. They were big travelers. They took at least three to four trips a year. They started taking me with them once I got older."

"Where have you been?" Alana asked.

"Mostly places throughout Europe. London, Paris, Rome, Athens, Berlin, Barcelona, Prague, Istanbul..."

"You guys did go places. The only place I've ever been other than the islands is California."

"Why didn't you ever hit Europe?" I asked.

"Didn't have the money."

"Where would be your top destination?"

"Paris, by far. I've always dreamed of seeing the Louvre, the Eiffel Tower, walking down the Champs-Elysees."

"We'll have to go sometime," I said.

"I still don't have the money."

I didn't say anything. I didn't want to tell her that I'd cover the costs because I wasn't sure if that would sound like I was bragging. Alana put the photo album back on the table.

"How do you think this turns out?" she asked.

"I think whoever wrote that note is going to get freaked out once they see the security team show up. They'll probably drop the matter. It will take time, but Mrs. Chambers will eventually get over it."

"I hope you're right," Alana said.

5

THE SWIMMING POOL

THE SECURITY TEAM ARRIVED AT SEVEN. ALANA SHOWED THEM AROUND the house and gave them instructions. Patricia came downstairs just as Alana finished talking to the two security officers. She looked exhausted, and I guessed she'd spent most of the night staring at the ceiling and wondering who would want to hurt her boss.

"Mrs. Chambers is still sleeping," Patricia said.

I assumed she'd anticipated the question.

Alana introduced the security team to Patricia. I'd hoped their presence would make her feel somewhat better, but she didn't act like it. She just stared at the floor the entire time they talked to her. Alana thanked the team again, and they walked away to take up their posts.

"Are you going to be all right? Do you need me to stay longer?" I asked Patricia.

"No, I'll be fine." She turned to Alana. "Thanks for getting those guys."

"It's no problem."

"May I have the two wine bottles Mrs. Chambers selected so I can have them tested?" I asked.

Patricia left for the kitchen and returned with the bottles. She handed them to me.

"Thank you. I'll be back in a few hours to speak with Mrs. Chambers," I said.

Patricia nodded and walked us to the door.

"Call me if you need anything before that," I said.

"Thanks."

Alana and I went outside just as Foxx pulled into the driveway. I'd texted him during the night after Alana had confirmed the arrival time of the security team. Foxx drove Alana to her house, and then we headed back to our home in Ka'anapali.

"Do you really think someone is trying to kill her?" Foxx asked as we pulled into the driveway.

"I don't know what to think," I admitted.

We went into the house, and Maui the dog ran up to us.

"I took him for a walk this morning right before I left to pick you guys up," Foxx said.

"Thanks."

I walked over to the sofa and plopped down.

"What's your next move?" Foxx asked.

"I'm going to ship those wine bottles off to a lab in Oahu. Alana gave me the address of the place they use. I don't think the pack-and-ship place opens for another hour, though."

"Use the time to rest. You can't think straight if you're this exhausted."

I closed my eyes for what I thought would be a few minutes. I woke up when Foxx shook me.

"What time is it?" I asked.

"You've been out for a few hours. I thought about letting you sleep even longer, but I figured you'd want to get started."

"Damn," I said.

I stood and stumbled back to the bathroom. I stripped off my clothes and climbed into the shower. I hoped the cold water would wake me, but it didn't really help that much. I got dressed, grabbed the wine bottles, and drove to the store to ship them off. After I left the store, I called Alana.

"How's it going?" I asked.

"I feel like a zombie. What about you?"

"The same. Any news on Mrs. Chambers?"

"I was just about to head over there," Alana said.

"Mind if I meet you there?"

"Not at all."

I ended the call and got into my car. I put the top down because I thought the wind would help me wake up; it didn't. The sun was bright, and it was already starting to get hot, which made me even more tired. I saw Alana's car when I parked along the curb in front of Mrs. Chambers' house. Alana exited the front door. I climbed out of my car, and we met at about the halfway point on the driveway. I could instantly tell something was wrong by the look on Alana's face.

"You're not going to believe this," Alana said.

"What happened?"

"Mrs. Chambers released the security detail, and she's left the house. No one knows where to, and no one's talking."

"What?"

"She told the security guys they weren't needed."

"Did they call you?" I asked.

"No, and I just got off the phone chewing their asses off about that. They said they were instructed not to inform me, and since I wasn't the one paying them, they couldn't go against their client's wishes."

"What about Patricia?" I asked.

"I couldn't get anything out of her."

"This is absurd."

I walked past Alana and headed toward the house. Patricia opened the front door before I could knock.

"I know what you're going to ask me, and I'm sorry, but Mrs. Chambers specifically told me not to call you."

"When did she leave?" I asked.

Patricia said nothing. I really didn't know how to respond to her silence. It was infuriating, and my fatigue only made the situation worse. I wanted to walk back to my car, drive home, climb into bed, and sleep for a couple of days straight. What was the point in trying to help someone who apparently no longer wanted your help? Unfortunately, by this time, I felt a certain obligation to assist Mrs. Chambers. I couldn't just walk away.

"You realize she's in danger. You saw the note last night," I said.

Patricia still said nothing.

"Did she even tell you when she'd be back?" Alana asked.

Patricia shook her head.

"So you're really not going to say anything? Your employer's life is in danger, and you're apparently okay with keeping your mouth shut?" I asked.

"Do you think I wanted any of this to happen? I don't know where she went. I don't know when she'll be back. I know nothing except she wanted her plans to be kept secret, even from me."

"There's nothing we can do," Alana told me.

"Can you put out a BOLO for her car?" I asked.

"I could, but the lady doesn't want to be found. She apparently left of her own accord. She's committed no crimes. We can't force her to come back. We can't keep her locked up in her home."

I knew Alana was right. Mrs. Chambers' behavior made no sense to me, but it was her decision, not mine. I turned to Patricia.

"Will you at least call us when she comes back?"

Patricia said nothing. She turned and walked back into the house. Alana and I waited another minute, and I did my best to breathe and return my blood pressure to normal. We walked back to Alana's car.

"Look. I'll unofficially call a few people who I know are on patrol today. I'll ask them to look for the car. It can't hurt."

I nodded. "So what now?" I asked.

"I go back to the office, and you go home."

It seemed like a lousy plan, but it wasn't like we had any better options. I hugged Alana goodbye and got back into my car. I watched her drive away.

I tried to figure out who else might know the whereabouts of Mrs. Chambers. I considered calling one of her children but quickly dismissed the idea since the prevailing theory was one of them was responsible for the threats. I thought about Mara. She was the one who got me involved with this in the first place. Maybe she'd heard from Mrs. Chambers. I pulled out my cell phone and called Mara. Her assistant connected me.

"Mara, this is Poe. I don't suppose you've heard from Mrs. Chambers today."

"No, I haven't spoken to her since last night."

I quickly brought her up to speed.

"I don't know where she could have gone," Mara admitted.

"You don't happen to have a cell phone number for her?"

"I don't even know if she has a cell phone. I only have a home number."

"Does she have an office somewhere? I remember her children telling me she was still involved with the business."

"I believe she has one at the hotel."

"I'll give it a shot. I'll let you know if I find her."

I ended the call and started the car. I thought the hotel was only about ten minutes from the house. If she wasn't in her office, I would poke my nose around and see if anyone had seen her that morning.

The hotel was closer than I thought. It took me a grand total of four minutes of driving time down the coast. It was easy to see why the larger hotel corporations would want to snatch this property up. It was right across from a gorgeous beach. You would be hard-pressed to find a nicer location on this part of the island.

The hotel was around fifty years old. I wish I could say it had an older elegance to it, maybe something that captured the style and grace of the house Millard Chambers had designed on a restaurant napkin. Unfortunately, it didn't. It was rather plain, but it was well kept. The paint looked relatively fresh, and the grounds were clean and well-groomed. The parking lot was full, so at least it was good to know they were still doing decent business. Maybe they kept their rates lower than the competition. That, and the Wailea location, could be more than enough to keep attracting customers for years to come.

I parked my car and walked into the lobby. It was large and had an open-air design that allowed the cool ocean breezes to blow throughout. I spotted the door to the administrative offices behind the front desk. I waited a minute while the desk clerk finished checking in a family of four. She eventually handed them their room keys, and they wheeled their luggage away.

"Hello," I said. "I was wondering if you could tell me if Mrs. Charlotte Chambers is in her office today?"

"No, I haven't seen her, but that's not unusual. We don't see her here that much."

"I don't suppose you have a cell phone number for her?" I asked.

"I'm afraid we aren't allowed to give information like that out."

"Of course," I said.

I just stood another minute at the front desk. I wasn't sure what to do next. I was wondering if I should just throw my hands up and go home when Mill Chambers walked out of the office. He immediately recognized me. I didn't know if that was a good thing or not.

"Poe, what are you doing here?" he asked.

"I came by to have lunch with your mother," I said.

The lie just flew out of my mouth, and I didn't even consciously recall thinking about it before spitting it out. I went into a minor panic as I realized I wasn't even sure if they had an on-site restaurant. Many hotels did, but this was an older one, and I didn't know if they'd made the investment.

"That's odd. My mother usually has her lunch dates at the house," he said.

"Well, she also promised me a tour of the hotel," I said, and the lies kept getting deeper and deeper.

"Sounds like you two really hit it off. Let me give her a call and see where she's at."

Mill removed a cell phone from his front pocket and dialed his mother. There were two potential outcomes, and neither was good for me. Option one was she didn't answer the phone, and I'd be no closer to discovering where she was. Option two was she'd answer the phone and inform her son that I'd just lied to him. I thought about both options as the phone continued to ring. I couldn't decide which one I wanted to unfold.

"Hey, Mom, it's me. Your lunch guest is waiting here in the lobby. Give me a call and let me know how late you're running. Bye."

Mill ended the call and slipped the phone back in his pocket.

"Is there anything I can get you while you wait?" he asked.

"No, I'm good. Thanks for calling her. I'm a little early, so maybe I'll just take a short walk around the property and then come back to the lobby."

"Can I show you around?"

"No, no. I'm good," I said.

"Okay, but don't hesitate to ask if you need anything."

I shook hands with Mill, and he walked away. The desk clerk eyed me. I knew she didn't buy the lunch story, but I also knew she had no way of guessing what was really going on. I looked around the lobby for a few more seconds, and then walked toward the back of the property in case Mill was still watching me and wondering why I hadn't started my self-guided tour.

I quickly came upon a large pool behind the hotel. It was several times the size of the one behind Mrs. Chambers' home. There were about twenty guests in and around it. I circled the area. There were several neatly manicured bushes and flower beds that enclosed the area and lined the building. Again, it wasn't the nicest property I'd ever seen, but it was well cared for. I didn't know much about the hotel business, practically nothing, actually, but judging by the crowds I saw, the Chambers family had to have been making a decent living off this place.

I walked back to the lobby. Mill wasn't around, and the desk clerk was busy with another family. I left the lobby and walked back to my car. I called Alana along the way.

"I don't suppose anyone's seen her car?" I asked.

"Nothing. Any news on your end?"

"No, nothing here either."

I told Alana about my call to Mara and my trip to the hotel.

"So Mill didn't seem concerned about anything?" Alana asked.

"No, the guy acted like he didn't have a care in the world."

"This just gets weirder by the minute. Call me if something changes. I've got to go."

I ended the call and climbed into the convertible. The traffic was heavy, and it took me over an hour to get home. I was exhausted, and the hot sun beating down left me feeling cranky. Foxx was gone when I got back, which was probably a good thing. I hate being around others when those moods strike.

I let Maui the dog out back with me, and I stripped off my shirt and shoes and dove into the swimming pool. I swam underwater the length of the pool. When I came to the surface and wiped the water out of my eyes, I saw Maui standing at the edge staring at me. I'm pretty sure dogs can tell when their owners aren't feeling well.

I climbed out of the pool and walked over to a chair. The dog followed me. I leaned over and scratched the top of his head. Then I plopped down on the chair. It wasn't the most comfortable thing, but I accomplished something for the first time in my life. I actually fell asleep sitting up straight. I awoke for the second time that day with Foxx shaking me.

"You all right?" he asked.

I said nothing and rubbed my eyes.

"Damn, buddy. I thought you'd had a heart attack and died. How did you sleep with your head slumped over like that?"

"What time is it?" I asked.

"It's after seven. How long have you been back?"

"I'm not sure. I don't remember when I got back exactly."

"You ever find that lady?"

"No, she apparently doesn't want to be found."

I stood, and we both walked inside, Maui the dog following us. I went into the kitchen and poured myself a glass of water. I was drenched in sweat from sleeping in the sun for so long. I gulped the water down and poured myself a second glass.

"I'm sure she's okay. This just sounds like a greedy child or two trying to scare their mother into selling the place off."

"Maybe," I said.

I wasn't even sure why I'd become so obsessed with the case, though I thought I knew why. I had thoroughly dismissed Charlotte Chambers when I met her in Mara's office. I'd viewed her as a crazy old lady. It's true that we all make snap judgments that are often incredibly unfair, and there was really no positive thing to come from me beating myself up about it, but I had essentially laughed off her concerns. The threatening note changed all of that, and I really wanted to do my best to make things up to her. I couldn't, though. She obviously no longer wanted my help.

I drank the second glass of water and ate a banana. I followed Foxx into the living room, and we watched a show about aliens being responsible for all the great accomplishments throughout history, such as the pyramids and the Sphinx. It was mindless television, but that's what my brain needed at that moment. I was tempted to go to sleep again, but I knew I needed to get my body clock back on track. The episode ended and another began. This one was about Bigfoot really being an offspring of an extraterrestrial. I was saved from watching it when the doorbell rang. Maui barked and took off running toward the door. I pried myself off the sofa and walked to the front of the house. I gazed through the peep hole and saw Alana. I opened the door.

"Man, you look so much better than I do. I've slept twice today and still feel like I'm about to fall over," I said.

"Trust me. I'm not far behind you. I'm running on pure adrenaline right now."

Alana bent over and patted the dog. "Hey there, Maui."

He wagged his tail in appreciation.

Alana and I walked back into the living room.

"How's it going?" Foxx asked.

"Long day. I'd love to sit down, but I don't think I'd be able to get back up," she said.

"You want something to drink?" I asked her.

"I'd love a beer," she said.

"I'll take one too," Foxx said.

I walked into the kitchen and pulled two beers out of the refrigerator. My cell phone vibrated on the kitchen counter as I walked back into the living room. I handed the beers to Alana and Foxx, and then dashed back to the kitchen to grab the phone before the call ended. I didn't recognize the number on the display.

"Hello," I said.

"Poe, this is Patricia."

I wasn't sure how to respond. This was the lady who refused to talk earlier and now she was calling me?

"Mrs. Chambers returned home about twenty minutes ago."

"Is she okay?" I asked.

"She seemed fine, a bit grumpy, but fine."

"May I speak with her?"

"I'm not at the house any longer. She told me to leave."

"I assume she gave you her permission to call me and tell me she was all right," I said.

"Not exactly. She told me not to come back to work until she contacted me."

"Why would she say that?"

"I don't know. We've always gotten along fine. I care for her. I don't know why she would send me away without an explanation. I'm sorry I couldn't tell you anything this morning, but I just wanted you to know she was home."

"Thanks for the call," I said.

"Was that Patricia?" Alana asked.

I nodded and relayed the conversation.

"That makes no sense," Alana said.

"None of this does. Do we take a trip over there?"

"I don't feel like it, but I think we should."

We said goodbye to Foxx and headed outside.

"I'll drive. It looks like you're about to pass out," Alana said.

The traffic was much lighter than my last drive. We got there in about fifty minutes. I called Charlotte Chambers a couple of times on the way over and got no response, not even a voicemail or answering machine.

It was dark by the time we arrived. We drove up to the house, and I recognized Charlotte Chambers' car from the last time I saw it outside Mara's office. Alana parked on the street, and we made our way to the front door.

"See that?" I asked.

I motioned to the front door. It was slightly ajar.

Alana slid her foot against the bottom of the door and pushed it open.

"Mrs. Chambers," she called out.

There was no response.

Alana stepped a foot inside the house.

"Mrs. Chambers," she said again.

Still nothing.

Alana turned to me.

"Stay behind me."

She removed her gun and went farther inside. I stayed behind her as she requested. Sometimes it's tough dating a detective. The male side of you has the instinct of protecting the woman. I'm sorry if that sounds chauvinistic to you female readers, but it's the truth. On the other hand, Alana had a lot more training than me, and she was armed. Plus, I'd displayed a tendency to get myself seriously hurt on my two previous investigations. I'm sure Alana was tired of visiting me in the hospital.

The house was completely dark. We made our way into the living room. Alana found a switch on the wall and flipped on the lights. Charlotte Chambers was nowhere to be seen.

"Mrs. Chambers, this is Detective Alana Hu. Are you home?"

"Should we try upstairs?" I asked.

Alana nodded. I followed her up the stairs to the master bedroom. The bed was made. Everything looked perfectly normal, but there was no Mrs. Chambers to be found. We checked the other bedrooms, no one.

"Maybe she went outside," I suggested. "There's a large window in the bedroom that overlooks the backyard."

We walked back into her bedroom and made our way over to the window. It was too dark outside to see anything, but then I noticed a large light switch beside the window. Each switch was labeled. I hit the one that read "backyard." Multiple lights instantly turned on, including the lights to the swimming pool. It took all of two seconds for me to spot the body. It was surrounded by long, flowing streaks of red. It looked like she was floating in a setting sun.

"Damn," I said.

I'd gotten to the window before Alana had, and I rushed past her.

"Poe, wait," she called after me.

I ran down the stairs, through the living room, and out the sliding glass door that led to the back patio. I dove into the pool and swam over to the body. I turned it upside down and confirmed it was Charlotte Chambers. I dragged her unconscious body over to the side of the pool. Alana pulled while I lifted the body. Alana gently laid Mrs. Chambers on her back. I climbed out of the red-soaked pool while Alana started CPR. She did it for a full two minutes. There was no response, no coughing, no sign of life. Alana looked up at me. I didn't know what to say, so I said nothing.

Alana pulled out her phone and called in the report. Two police cars and an ambulance arrived within twenty minutes. I sat beside Charlotte Chambers' body the entire time. I didn't want her to be alone. I know that may sound silly, and maybe even pointless, but I felt responsible. I should have taken the case more seriously. I never should have doubted her. The woman was dead. I didn't know if it was over a piece of beachfront property or not. Maybe there was a much deeper mystery going on, and I vowed there on the patio beside the swimming pool that I would find out who did this.

The paramedics lifted the body onto a stretcher and wheeled it out to the ambulance. The police taped off the area. Alana told me I needed to wait out by her car. By this point, most of the neighbors had come out of their houses. The local media arrived about thirty minutes later. I guessed one of the neighbors called them. Judging by the large turnout she'd had at the party, I knew Charlotte Chambers was a high-profile member of the community. Her death would be big news.

The next couple of days were a blur. Alana got the case as I expected, and she was good enough to keep me informed of her progress, even though I hadn't physically seen her since the discovery of the body in the pool.

She'd called Mill and his wife and Bethany and her husband. None of them took the news well, but that was to be expected. Even if one of them had been responsible for the death, it wasn't like they were going to celebrate in front of Alana. She wasn't able to reach Joe Chambers, the youngest child who Foxx saw snorting drugs at the party. Mill told Alana that wasn't unusual because Joe had a habit of not returning phone calls.

The autopsy revealed Charlotte Chambers had been struck on the back of the head with a large object with a thin edge, maybe something like a shovel. The blow had opened a vicious cut, which was the cause of all of the blood in the swimming pool. The body was then either pushed into the water, or Charlotte simply fell into the swimming pool after being hit so hard. There was no way to tell if Charlotte immediately died from the blow to the head or if she had drowned first. The way I saw it, it didn't really matter. The woman was dead.

6

JOE CHAMBERS

I COULDN'T STOP THINKING ABOUT THE MOMENT I SPOTTED CHARLOTTE Chambers' body floating in the pool. When I looked out the second-story window, I knew it was her without having seen her face. I couldn't imagine what her last seconds of life had been like, the water rushing into her mouth and down her throat, filling her lungs. It had to have been beyond horrifying. Who could have done that to an elderly woman, or anyone for that matter? I desperately wanted to help with the case, but Alana told me they had it under control. It wasn't under control, though. The killer or killers were still walking free. The media was having a field day after someone, presumably at the police department, let slip the gory details of the murder. A grisly cell phone photo appeared the next day. It didn't feature the body, but it prominently showed the streaks of blood in the pool. Mara Winters was furious, and the leaks only served to solidify her distrust of the police department.

Charlotte Chambers' adult children, with the exception of Joe, demanded to know why Alana never informed them of the threatening note left in their mother's pantry. Alana was playing defense when she should have been on the offensive. No, there was nothing controlled about the situation at all, but there I sat on the sidelines, twiddling my thumbs and spinning my wheels and any other clichéd saying I could think of to reinforce the notion that I wasn't allowed to do anything.

Mara Winters called me the day before the funeral, and everything about my involvement changed. She asked me to meet her at her favorite sushi restaurant. We spoke about Charlotte Chambers. Mara told me a few stories. They were mostly little embarrassing tales that we all find ourselves in from time to time, but they made me laugh, which always makes one feel good. Toward the end of the lunch, I sensed Mara was struggling with something. I didn't think it likely she had invited me to lunch just to tell meaningless stories. The sushi was nice, but it wasn't that nice, if you get my meaning.

We paid the tab, and I walked Mara to her car. She opened her door but hesitated a moment before climbing in.

"What's bothering you? You want to tell me something, right?" I asked.

"It's called not violating attorney-client confidentiality."

"Is it something Charlotte told you?"

"No."

I said nothing. I thought it best to let her decide how far she wanted to go.

"I got a visit from Joe Chambers this morning."

If I could have raised just one eyebrow, I would have.

"Did you know Alana's been unable to get a hold of him for the last few days?" I asked.

"No, but that doesn't really surprise me."

"What did he want?"

"That's not something I can divulge," Mara said.

"Do you want me to guess?" I asked.

"If you hit the mark, which you won't, I couldn't even acknowledge if you were right or not."

"You've got to give me something," I said.

"You're right. I do. I've been keeping this in my pocket the entire lunch, trying to decide if I was willing to even go this far."

Mara reached into her pocket and removed a small piece of paper. She handed it to me.

"What's this?" I asked.

"It's Joe Chambers' address. I think you or Alana should pay him a visit. He has big news."

Mara climbed inside her car without saying another word. She started the engine and drove off. I watched her leave the parking lot and then looked down at the address. He lived in Kihei. Do you remember when I spoke about defining moments? You either turn left or you turn right? Well, this was another one of those decisions. Did I call Alana or not? If I called, she'd probably tell me to stay away and she'd go speak with Joe herself. If I didn't call and discovered valuable information on my own, I'd have to tell her about it. She'd be furious with me. Sure, she'd eventually get over it, but maybe she'd never trust me again with these cases. So I did what any sensible man would do in the situation. I caved into the fear of getting read the riot act. I called Alana.

"Hello," she said.

"I have a little piece of information I think you might be interested in, but I need you to make me a promise first."

"Is this one of those times you want me to promise not to get mad? Because I won't."

"No, nothing like that. In all fairness, she came to me."

"Who came to you? What have you been up to?"

"Mara. She didn't exactly give me information. She just pointed me in the right direction."

"And what direction would that be?" Alana asked.

"Here's the deal. I want to go with you. I can't be on the sidelines. It's driving me crazy."

"So this is deal-making time now?"

"Don't look at it like that. You know I'm bluffing. You know I'm going to tell you regardless of what you say."

"Is this your way of begging without actually having to beg?" she asked.

"Something like that."

"Spit it out."

I told Alana about my lunch with Mara and her suggestion that Alana or I check out Joe Chambers.

"He has big news," Alana repeated Mara's last line to me.

"I have no idea what it is, but I'm sure Mara wouldn't have contacted me if it wasn't potentially important to the case."

"Give me ten minutes. I'll call you back."

Alana hung up. I thought about sitting in the car and waiting for her to call, but I decided to gamble that she wouldn't say no. I started the car and pointed it toward Kihei. Alana called me back in about twenty minutes.

"Hello," I said.

"Is that wind I hear?"

"Why do you ask?"

"Because I'm wondering if you're driving to Joe Chambers' house right now."

"Not exactly."

"So where exactly are you going?"

"To that chain restaurant in Kihei. I thought I'd order chicken fingers and a Long Island Iced Tea while I awaited your decision."

Alana laughed. "I spoke to the captain. I told him you've been working as a private investigator, and you've been on this case for weeks. I suggested it would be better for you to be working with us than on your own. He reluctantly agreed. Consider yourself an unpaid consultant on this, at least for the time being. He could change his mind at any point."

"Understood. Do I get one of those junior badges?"

"Be serious, Poe. This is a big deal. I really stuck my neck out for you."

"I know you did, and I appreciate it. I won't let you down."

"I'll meet you at the restaurant, and lay off the Long Islands."

Alana and I met in the parking lot of the restaurant with the first word that starts with an *r* and the second word that starts with a *t*. I turned my car off and climbed into hers.

"Any guess what this big news is?" Alana asked.

"Not a clue. I'm not even sure how we get it out of him and not bring up Mara in the conversation," I said.

"That's if he's even at home. I left the guy several messages. Who knows where he is."

We arrived at Joe Chambers' home after a short drive from the restaurant. He lived a few blocks from the beach in a house that was considerably smaller than his mother's, but he had a beautiful red Mercedes parked in the driveway. It was a similar model to my two-seater, but the Mercedes was probably a good twenty to thirty grand more. The guy clearly wasn't hurting for money.

"Have we gotten lucky? Is he actually home?" I asked.

"Maybe."

Alana parked behind the Mercedes, and we walked to the front door. She rang the doorbell, and we waited a good minute with no response. She rang the doorbell a second time. We waited another minute before I heard footsteps inside. Joe Chambers opened the door. I hadn't seen him at the party, but I recognized him and his glorious hair from the photo his mother sent me. I had been right before. He did get all the looks in the family. He looked absolutely nothing like the rather ordinary Mill or Bethany.

"Mr. Chambers?" Alana asked.

Joe nodded.

"My name's Detective Alana Hu. This is my associate, Mr. Ruther-ford. May we come in and speak with you?"

I thought it was kind of cool that she referred to me in that way. I thought I might start introducing myself as Alana's associate at parties.

Joe nodded a second time and turned away from us. He left the door open and walked back toward what I assumed was a living room. He didn't say "Sure, come on in," or "Right this way, please." It was rather odd, and I wondered if the guy was high given Foxx's earlier encounter with him. The place was dark. All of the curtains had been pulled shut. The television was on, but the sound was muted. There were a grand total of four pizza boxes sitting on the table in front of the sofa. Empty beer cans were placed around the boxes. Some of the cans had fallen to the floor. It reminded me of the aftermath of a frat party.

Joe sat on the sofa. He didn't invite us to sit. There really wasn't anywhere for us to sit, anyway, except beside him on the sofa, which I had no desire to do. I was tempted to say "Nice place," but I knew I'd never be able to disguise the sarcasm in my voice.

"My condolences on the loss of your mother," Alana said.

"Yeah, it stinks."

"When did you find out? I wasn't able to reach you."

"My brother left me a message. Can you believe that? He didn't even have the decency to tell me in person."

I thought about saying that I understood Mill's predicament, considering Joe obviously didn't bother to return phone calls.

"I didn't know your mother very well, but from the few times we interacted, she seemed like a remarkable woman," I said.

Joe nodded.

"Do you know of anyone who might have wanted to hurt your mother?" Alana asked.

"Mill said you were investigating it as a crime. Is that what happened? Someone pushed her into that pool?"

"We think so."

I wasn't sure if Joe had heard about the deadly blow to his mother's head. Maybe Mill hadn't told him, or maybe he had, but Joe didn't remember the details because he was drunk when the news was relayed. "Did she tell you about anyone threatening her?" I asked.

"No, she never said anything."

"Did Mill ever mention anything to you about threats to your mother?" Alana asked.

"Mill and I don't really talk."

"I thought you both work at the hotel," I said.

"We do. I'm a bartender in the restaurant at night. He works the day shift. We manage to avoid each other." Then Joe did something I found incredibly weird and slightly disturbing. He laughed. It wasn't one of those small laughs one does when hearing a slightly amusing joke. This was a huge, side-splitting belly laugh.

"Wait until he finds out. I can't wait to see the look on his face," Joe said.

My conversation with Mara Winters popped into my head. This had to be the news she vaguely referenced.

"Until he finds out what?" Alana asked.

"That son of a bitch had it coming. My whole life he's put me down," Joe said.

"Who has? Mill?" I asked.

"He doesn't think I'm worthy of the Chambers name, as if that name means anything, anyway." Joe laughed again. "He's going to shit himself. Bethany will, too."

I wasn't sure if this guy was just deranged or if my earlier guess that he was high was indeed correct. Neither Alana nor I said anything. We just waited for Joe to stop laughing.

"They couldn't wait for her to die. Did they tell you that? Of course they didn't," Joe said.

"Who wanted her to die?" Alana asked.

"My brother and sister. They wanted her dead."

"You heard them say that?" Alana asked.

"No, they would never be that obvious, but I knew. You know how old my grandmother was when she passed? Ninety-nine years old. She was three months shy of turning one hundred. Can you believe that? Three lousy months!"

I wasn't sure why he'd just brought up his grandmother, unless he was implying his siblings didn't expect their mother to go anytime soon. Did that mean one of them wanted to speed things up by drowning her in a pool?

"Your mother told me she'd received an offer to sell the hotel to a large hospitality corporation. Is that true?" I asked.

"Yeah, she showed me the offer."

He laughed again.

"What's so funny about the offer?" Alana asked.

"She left it to me. She left it all to me," Joe said. He laughed again. I thought he might fall off the sofa.

I moved closer to Alana. "I think we got what we came for," I whispered.

"Absolutely." Alana turned back to Joe. "Mr. Chambers, we'd like to express our condolences again. If you think of anything we should know that will aid us in our investigation, please call."

Alana removed a business card from her pocket and placed it on the table beside the beer cans and empty pizza boxes. Joe didn't respond. He was still too busy laughing.

Alana and I let ourselves out. We didn't say anything to each other until we got inside her car.

"You think it's true?" Alana asked.

"One way to find out," I said.

I pulled out my phone and called Mara Winters. I didn't want to put the phone on speaker. She would have been able to tell, and I didn't want it to freak her out to think I was broadcasting this conversation to the world, so I motioned for Alana to get close to me so she could hear.

"Mara, it's Poe."

"Judging by the excitement in your voice, I'm guessing you were able to talk to Joe."

"Are you able to tell me if Mrs. Chambers had a will?"

"Yes, she had one."

"Did Joe Chambers come by your office to get that will read to him today?"

"No, the contents of the will would have been divulged to the entire family at a specific time. I can't just show it to whoever pops in the office."

"Would have been?" I asked.

Mara hesitated a moment. "You're very observant."

"Or maybe you're just good at giving me clues. Joe showed up this morning with a new will, one that leaves him everything," I said.

"He told you that?" Mara asked.

"Not exactly. It's a guess on my part. You seemed bothered by your conversation with him, which leads me to believe you didn't know about his mother leaving him the estate. You were bound to know the contents of the original will, so I'm assuming there must have been a new one you didn't know existed."

"I can't confirm or deny that."

"Thanks, Mara. I understand."

I ended the call and turned to Alana.

"Did you hear all that?" I asked.

"Everything. You think the new will is legit?"

"I'd say yes, or at least it initially appears that way to Mara, and I'm sure it caught her completely by surprise."

"If it's real, when did it get made?" Alana asked.

"Better yet, why did it get made? When I met with Charlotte Chambers and Mara, she told me she had to know who had threatened her because she didn't want to leave them anything."

"Does that mean she thought both Mill and Bethany were behind the letters?"

"She was gone all day after we left her house. Maybe she figured something out."

"And got killed for it," Alana said.

"Does that mean we scratch Joe Chambers off the list?" I asked.

"I'm not willing to take anyone off the list, not yet."

"What's next then?"

"The funeral is tomorrow. Is that right?" Alana asked.

"I think so."

"Theoretically everyone will be there interacting with each other."

"So we wait for the new will to emerge so Mill and Bethany can shit their pants. Is that how Joe put it?" I asked.

"I believe so, but will Joe even show up tomorrow? The guy seemed pretty out of it."

"I'd say yes. He seems to really have cared for his mother. Plus, I think he can't wait to shock Mill."

"You think he'd do it at a funeral?" Alana asked.

I didn't answer her. I was too busy thinking about Joe going to see Mara Winters and presenting her with a new will. His mother wasn't even in the ground yet, and he was already laying claim to her money and property.

7

FUNERALS, FIGHTS, AND CHEAP SCOTCH

THERE WAS A HUGE TURNOUT FOR THE FUNERAL, AS I EXPECTED THERE would be. The sun was shining, and there wasn't a cloud in the sky. It was a hot day, which felt even hotter since I was dressed in a dark suit. I'd brought it with me from Virginia. At the time, I felt rather silly for packing it. Foxx had told me khaki pants and a collared shirt were considered dressing up by Hawaiian standards. I'd paid a decent amount of money for the suit, though, so I didn't want to just give it away. I figured it would sit in the back of my closet at Foxx's house and might not ever make its way out of the dry cleaner's plastic bag. Here I was, though, pulling it out just a few months after moving to Maui.

I went to the funeral by myself. Alana didn't think it appropriate to mourn with the family when she was about to launch a full-scale investigation into those very same people.

I usually drove with the top down, but I decided to put it up and crank the air conditioner. It broke after blowing somewhat-cool air for a couple of minutes. I wasn't sure if I'd be cooler by keeping the top up to keep the sun off of me, or if the air flow from the top down would be better. Unfortunately, I was sitting in the long, slow funeral procession. There wasn't going to be much airflow today.

We all parked on the side of the main road that ran through the center of the cemetery. I got out of the car and walked to the burial plot. The funeral home had put up a small tent for the immediate family. Friends and acquaintances stood behind them. I stayed on the outskirts of the group. I was barely close enough to hear the minister.

I walked to the side of the crowd, so I could get a closer look at the family. I saw two young men sitting beside Mill and Jen. It was obvious they were their identical twin sons. One of them wore a black suit and the other was in a dark blue one. That was the only difference I could tell between them.

There was a woman about my age, maybe a few years older, sitting beside Bethany and Barry Williams. I guessed she was their daughter, Olivia.

Joe Chambers sat beside Olivia on the end of the front row. I knew he didn't have any children, and he hadn't brought anyone with him, at least no one he felt needed to sit with the family. I didn't know if it was obvious Joe was the outcast, or if I just had that impression because of what he'd told me during our interview the day before.

The minister was an older man, maybe in his early seventies. He spoke of Charlotte Chambers in general terms. The comments seemed taken out of some funeral-service template book. I guessed he didn't really know her. I wasn't sure if she'd been a religious person or not. It's possible he hadn't even met her before.

After the funeral, I drove to the Chambers Hotel for the wake. They held it in a large ballroom just off the lobby. It was a practical choice in terms of parking and size, but I wasn't sure how the vacationing guests would respond. Who wants to walk past a massive group of mourners all clad in black as you make your way to the pool to sunbathe and drink a pina colada?

I walked around the ballroom for several minutes and eventually ran into Patricia, Charlotte Chambers' personal assistant. She was standing alone in the corner of the room.

"How are you doing?" I asked.

"Not well. I just can't stop thinking about her. I still can't believe it happened. Have the police made any progress?"

"Not that I know of. What are you going to do now?" I asked.

"Mill offered me a job here at the hotel, but I don't think I'm going to take it."

"Why not?"

"It's in event planning, which I think I could handle. I certainly did enough of that for Mrs. Chambers to know what I'm doing, but I'm thinking of moving back to California."

"I didn't realize that is where you're from," I said.

"I grew up in southern California, but I came out to Maui a year ago with some friends. They eventually moved back, but I stayed since I had a good job with Mrs. Chambers."

"Are you getting island fever?"

"Somewhat. I love Maui, but I'm a bit tired of the slow pace."

"Is it okay if I ask you a few questions about Charlotte?"

"Sure."

"I was just wondering if any of her children have keys to her house?"

"They all did. They would just let themselves in when they came to visit. Sometimes I'd turn around, and they'd be there in the room with me. It always kind of freaked me out."

"Do you think it's odd they wouldn't knock?"

"Maybe not. I don't knock when I go see my parents, but I grew up in the house my parents live in."

"Did Charlotte drink wine every night before bed? I believe she told me that she did."

"Every night and every day at lunch. She usually went through a bottle a day. She always had the same brand, too. She was never willing to try anything new. Some of the restaurants she frequented would stock that wine just for her. She'd even bring her own bottle if she didn't think they had it."

"Is it a safe bet then that all of her kids knew her favored wine?" I asked.

"I don't see how they wouldn't. Anyone who was around her for more than a day or two would have picked up on it."

"Where did she get the wine? Did she buy it at the same store every time?"

"I would always buy it. I'd go grocery shopping for her once a week, on Monday mornings. She'd make a list for me, and a case of the wine was always the first thing on the list." Patricia laughed. "I told her I didn't need a list. It was always the same things, but she always insisted on giving me one."

"No family members ever showed up with a bottle?" I asked.

"Not that I ever saw. I guess that's not good for me since the wine was supposedly drugged, and I'm the one who always bought it."

She was right to a certain degree, but her alibi for the time of Charlotte's death was solid. I never seriously suspected her anyway. She had nothing to gain from Charlotte's murder.

"How was Mrs. Chambers when she returned to the house that day?"

"Like I told you before, she seemed fine. She was in a bit of a bad mood, but she often seemed like that. The hotel really stressed her out."

"Do you know why?" I asked.

"She'd always complain about how Mill and Bethany were running things. Actually, she never really complained to me directly. It was more like she was just talking to herself out loud, and I happened to hear."

"What would she say about them?"

"That Mill didn't know what he was doing, and Bethany couldn't sell. She was always complaining about Bethany and Barry not booking enough events."

"Did she ever talk to you about the offer she got on the hotel property?"

"No, I wasn't even aware she'd received an offer until this mess happened."

Patricia and I spoke for a few more minutes. I appreciated her willingness to help, but I didn't learn anything new beyond the fact all of Charlotte Chambers' children had a key to the house. It wasn't like they really needed one to do the deed anyway. She would have undoubtedly let them inside.

I left Patricia and went to the bar to get a drink. I ordered a scotch on the rocks and nursed it as I made my way around the room. It was actually quite harsh and burned the back of my throat. I didn't get a good look at the bottle when the bartender served, but I assumed they were serving the cheapest kind available. It was my own fault. Who orders scotch at a wake anyway?

I tried to make my way over to Mill and Jen or Bethany and Barry, but the four of them were constantly surrounded by well-wishers.

I finished about half of my drink and walked toward one of the corners of the room to place the glass on a large tray. I stood beside the tray for a few minutes and looked around the room until I spotted Joe Chambers talking to a thirty-something woman. She wore a black dress that looked a bit on the tight and short side. It wasn't exactly the most appropriate attire for a funeral. Joe whispered something in her ear and then walked away. I paused a moment and then approached her.

"Hello, I'm Poe. I'm a friend of Joe's."

"Hi, I'm Candi, with an i."

I paused a moment and then realized she was referring to her name ending with an i instead of a y. I wasn't sure why she felt the need to point that out, but to each their own.

"How do you know Joe?" I asked.

"We're dating," she said.

"That's nice," I said.

She smiled.

"Terrible thing about his mother, isn't it?" I asked.

"Yeah, it really sucks, but these things happen," Candi said.

I'd probably have choked on my bad scotch if I'd still been drinking it.

"How long have you known Joe?" she asked.

"Not that long. I really just met him for the first time the other day. We met at his mother's party."

"You're not really his friend then, are you?"

"No, I guess you could say we're more acquaintances than anything else."

Candi didn't say anything, and we both reached that awkward point in the conversation where we were trying to figure out an escape route without being obvious.

"I was wondering, Candi, if it would be okay for me to get your phone number? There are a few questions I'd like to ask you, but this isn't really the time or place."

Candi looked for Joe, but he'd disappeared into the crowd. I wasn't sure if she felt like she needed his approval before talking to me, but she told me her number, and I typed it into my phone.

"Give me a call anytime," she said.

Then Candi walked away. I assumed she left to go find Joe. I thought about going back to the bar and getting another drink, maybe a beer this time, but I decided not to. I needed a clear head for the drive home. I was deeply depressed and had no idea how to proceed with the case.

I walked around the room some more and saw who I assumed to be Olivia, the daughter of Bethany and Barry Williams. She looked nothing like her parents. Have you ever seen photos of models with their parents and sometimes the models are quite striking while the parents' looks leave a lot to be desired? A similar case could be made with Olivia's beauty. Whereas Bethany and Barry were rather round and plain, Olivia was slender and stunning. She was talking to another woman. I walked up to her after the woman had left.

"Are you Olivia Williams?" I asked.

"Yes."

"My name's Poe. My condolences on your loss."

"Thank you. How did you know my grandmother?"

"I worked briefly with her, long enough to be impressed by her."

Olivia nodded.

"I believe she mentioned to me that you are in the wedding-planning business. Is that correct?"

Before Olivia could answer, we heard a loud argument break out behind us. I turned and saw Mill Chambers shove his brother, Joe.

"You son of a bitch. You really think this is going to make a difference," Mill yelled.

Mill snatched a piece of paper out of Joe's hands and tore it in
half.

"Go ahead. I made copies. You can't tear them all up," Joe said,
and then he laughed. It was the same out-of-control laugh Alana and
I had witnessed at his house.

Mill tossed the two torn pieces of paper to the floor.

"Shut up. Shut the hell up," Mill ordered, but it only made Joe
laugh even more.

I wondered if Joe was drunk. Based on the way he was acting, my
guess was yes.

Mill pushed Joe a second time. This time Joe pushed back. Then
Mill punched Joe in the face. It wasn't a direct hit, and it didn't knock
Joe over. Joe tackled Mill, and they both fell to the ground. Jen
screamed, at least I thought it was Jen.

Three guys, none of whom I recognized, got involved and tried to
pull the two brothers apart. It was a pretty vicious fight. They were
both really going for blood. I used the chaotic opportunity as a
chance to take a sneak at the paper that was still on the floor. I
grabbed both pieces and walked several feet away from the crowd.
Fortunately, the tear was across the middle of the page, and it was
fairly easy to read. It was a photocopy of the new will as I suspected.
It was only one paragraph long - *Charlotte Chambers, being of sound
mind, declares that all of her possessions go to her son Joe Chambers. This
will is her final decree and replaces all other wills before it.*

Charlotte's signature was at the bottom, along with two witness
signatures. I immediately recognized one of the witness' names.
Candi with an i.

8

CANDI WITH AN I

I CALLED CANDI THE MORNING AFTER THE FUNERAL. I ASKED IF I COULD meet her, and she agreed. I called Alana to invite her to join me, but all I got was her voicemail. I left a message for her to call me and took off for Kihei.

Candi lived in an apartment complex a few miles from Joe's house. If I had to rate the complex, I'd give it one star. It wasn't a crack den by any means, but it wasn't the kind of place I'd expect Joe Chambers to be visiting. On the other hand, drugs do have a way of bringing people from different economic backgrounds together. Ah, drugs, the great equalizer.

I climbed the stairs to the second floor and knocked on Candi's door. She answered within a few seconds.

"Hey there," she said.

It was difficult to keep my eyes from going directly to her chest. She was wearing all black, maybe she was still in mourning, but her black shorts were quite short, as was her tank top. The only way she could have flashed more cleavage was if she hadn't been wearing a shirt at all.

I entered her apartment, and she led me over to a sofa. I sat down, and she sat beside me rather than on the chair off to the side. The inside of the apartment was sparsely furnished, but it was clean, thank God.

"I was hoping you would call me," she said.

"Thanks for seeing me on such short notice," I said.

"I hate to do this, honey, but we need to get the money part out of the way. I charge two hundred an hour."

I almost burst out laughing. Candi with an i was a prostitute. How in the hell did I not see that? I felt like I was in a sitcom where two people have a colossal miscommunication and hilarious situations ensue.

"I'm afraid you've misinterpreted my intentions, or maybe I should have done a better job of explaining what I wanted," I said.

"Are you into something weird?" she asked.

I paused for a second, wondering what "weird" things she thought I might be in to.

"I don't think I'm into anything weird," I said. "I actually didn't come here for that. I'd like to ask you a few questions about Joe."

"What? Is he in some kind of trouble?"

"Not that I know of."

"You don't find me attractive?" she asked, and she rubbed her hand across my leg.

I know that readers of my first two tales are well aware of the fact I am always honest, perhaps too honest. Nevertheless, I'm not about to stop that habit now even if it causes me some embarrassment. To say I was not tempted by Candi would not be an accurate statement. The woman had an incredible body, one that she was showing off with a skimpy outfit, and she was rubbing my leg. A guy would have to be dead to not feel something. I must admit that I did feel a certain stirring. However, I managed to lift her hand off my leg and maintain my dignity.

"It's not that. You're quite stunning, but I am deeply in love with Alana Hu. I could never betray her."

Candi said nothing. I knew she didn't care one iota about my commitment to Alana or any other woman for that matter. Right now, she was just thinking about the lost revenue and how quickly she could replace me with a real, paying customer.

"How about this? I feel quite bad for not making my trip here clearer. I'll pay you fifty dollars to ask a few questions."

Candi hesitated and then said, "Let me see the money."

Smart woman. I reached into my wallet and removed two twenties and a ten.

"What do you want to know?" she asked.

"How long have you known Joe Chambers?"

"About a year. He came to me a few times. Eventually, he asked me out. I never date my clients, but there was something about him."

Was it the potential for a big pay day? I asked myself.

"You and Joe are dating then?"

"Yeah, maybe for a few months."

"Does Joe ever talk about his brother and sister?"

"Sometimes. He says they hate him."

"Did he say why?"

"He doesn't know. He says they've hated him from the moment he was born."

"Joe produced a new will that leaves him all of his mother's assets. I believe I saw your signature on that will as a witness. Is that correct?"

"Yeah, I signed it."

"So you were there when his mother signed it too?"

"Yeah, I was there."

"And where did you do it? At Joe's house?"

"No, at the lawyer's."

"What lawyer? Mara Winters?" I asked.

"I don't know her. A friend of mine did it. He's a lawyer. He wrote the new will for Joe's mom."

"Was his name the second witness signature?" I asked.

Candi with an *i* didn't answer me. I was half-tempted to ask if this attorney was a client of hers or if he was the lawyer she used when she inevitably found herself arrested for her given occupation.

"What's his name?" I asked.

"Halverson. Dick Halverson."

"Where is Mr. Halverson's office?"

"In Kahului. Near the airport."

"So Mr. Halverson drew up the new will and you, Joe, and Charlotte Chambers were in his office to sign it?"

"That's right."

"Did Joe say why he used Mr. Halverson instead of the family's regular attorney?"

"He said his mom was worried the regular attorney would argue with her. She said she wanted to leave everything to Joe, and she didn't want anybody fighting her about it, especially some lawyer."

"How did Mrs. Chambers seem that day?"

"What do you mean?"

"Was she happy, stressed, sad?"

"She seemed okay to me."

"Was that the first time you'd met Joe's mother?" I asked.

"Yeah."

"One last question. What was she wearing that day?"

"I don't remember. I don't even remember what I was wearing."

"Thanks, Candi."

I handed her the money.

"I'll tell Joe you came by."

"Sure thing. Give him my best."

I stood, but Candi stayed on the sofa. I guess I'll show myself out, I thought. I walked to the door and left without looking back. I wondered if she was going to tell Joe about my questions or if she was going to lead him to believe we engaged in her age-old profession. Either way, I assumed I was going to be getting a phone call from him in the near future.

I thought about calling Alana and filling her in on the details, but I decided to take a quick trip to Halverson's office first. I Googled his business and got the address in Kahului. The traffic was light, and I made good time. Halverson's place was tucked in the back of a one-story office building. There was no sign above his door. I circled the building and checked out the other businesses. Most of them had generic-sounding names that gave no clue as to what they actually did or sold, and I really couldn't get a good feel for the place. I parked on the opposite side of the building from Halverson's office and walked around to his door. It was made of glass, so it was easy to see inside. There was no receptionist and no name of a law firm on the wall like "Halverson, Halverson, and Halverson." There were no generic paintings with captions like *Courage* and *Teamwork*, no chairs in the lobby, and no plastic plants covered in dust.

I decided to go inside anyway. A little bell jingled as I opened the door.

"Can I help you?" I heard a male voice from one of the back rooms.

"Yes, I'm looking for Dick Halverson."

A few seconds later, Dick Halverson appeared. He was in his forties, a bit overweight and balding. He wore a pair of black pants and a polo shirt. It wasn't the kind of attire I was used to seeing attorneys wear, but then again, this was Hawaii.

"What can I do for you?" he asked.

"A friend of mine recently got arrested for drunk driving. He's in need of an attorney."

"A friend? Are we talking about you?" Halverson smiled.

"No, it's a friend. I live with the guy. He's pretty panicked, as I'm sure you can understand."

"How did you hear about me?"

"A lady I go to sometimes recommended you," I said.

"Ah, got yah," he said, and he pointed at me and laughed.

I wasn't sure if Halverson thought I was talking about Candi when I mentioned who had referred him to me, or if there were several other ladies of the same profession he represented. As a side note, I found it rather strange that he hadn't invited me back to his office. We were essentially conducting business in an empty room. This guy came across as more of a used car salesman than a lawyer. Of course, sometimes those two professions can attract the same kinds of personalities. Forgive me if you are, in fact, an attorney and are reading this tale for enjoyment. I'm sure you're of the upstanding kind and could never be confused for one peddling pre-owned vehicles.

"Is your friend still in jail?" he asked.

"No, they let him out on bail. This is his second arrest, though, and he's concerned he'll be heading off to jail for a year or two. He really needs an attorney to represent him."

"Where is he now? Why hasn't he come to see me?"

"The guy's a basket case. I can't even get him out of the house."

"I understand."

Halverson reached into his pocket and removed a business card.

"When he's ready to talk, have him give me a call." He handed me the card.

"There's one more thing, and I'm not sure how to approach this subject with you. Neither my friend nor I have a lot of money. If we were to pay you in cash, under the table so to speak, is there any way we could get a break on your rate?"

"That would be illegal, and I could get into a lot of trouble with the IRS."

"Okay, I understand. I hope I didn't insult you."

Halverson didn't reply, and I turned and walked toward the door.

"Have him call me. I'm sure we can work something out," he said.

"I will. Thanks."

I walked back to the other side of the office building and climbed into my car. I started the engine and drove out of the office complex. It took me about forty-five minutes to get home. Maui the dog greeted me as usual. I grabbed his leash, and we headed out the door. I called Alana while the dog and I walked around the neighborhood.

"Hey, I was just about to call you," she said.

"Yeah, you have some interesting news?" I asked.

"Not really. How did your meeting with Candi go?"

"You got my message?"

"Sorry I haven't called back sooner," she said. "It's been pretty hectic here."

"No problem." I filled Alana in on my visits with Candi and Dick Halverson.

"She thought you were there for sex?" Alana asked.

"It was rather awkward," I admitted.

"She's lucky I'm not the jealous type. I could have her place raided."

Don't let Alana fool you; all women are the jealous type.

"What was your impression of this lawyer?" Alana asked.

"He's an ambulance chaser, maybe even lower than that. I can't possibly see Charlotte Chambers using him for anything."

"Maybe it wasn't Charlotte's idea. It sounds like Joe set up the whole thing, and all she had to do was show up and sign the thing."

"Possibly," I said.

"Joe Chambers dates a prostitute. I wonder what his mother thought of that," Alana said.

"I don't think she had any idea. Candi said she only met Charlotte once, and that was at the lawyer's office when they supposedly signed the new will."

"Supposedly? You think it's a fake?" Alana asked.

"I'm not sure, but I asked Candi what Charlotte was wearing to the meeting, and she didn't remember. I'd have thought she'd have been nervous about meeting Joe's mom for the first time. I'd think she'd remember every detail."

"Maybe not. People are notorious for having bad memories. Ten people can see the same thing and remember it ten different ways."

"How late are you working? Want to do dinner tonight?" I asked.

"Sure. Your place or mine?"

"Why don't you come over to Foxx's," I suggested.

"Okay, I'll give you a call when I'm leaving."

I hung up and immediately called Mara Winters. I was on hold for several minutes. I wondered if she was neck-deep in matters involving the Chambers family.

"Hello, this is Mara Winters."

"Hey, Mara. This is Poe."

"What can I do for you?"

"I'm interested in creating a will for myself, and I was wondering if you could give some basic guidelines about what makes one valid."

"You know I can't talk specifics about my clients," she said.

"I get that, and I'm not going to ask for details, but I do have some general questions that would help me understand the situation better."

"What are they?" Mara asked.

"What makes a will valid? I'm sure there are certain things you need."

"It varies from state to state, but in Hawaii you generally need two witness signatures. There are several exceptions, for example, a holographic will."

"What's that?"

"It's when the person handwrites their entire will and signs it."

"And that would make a valid will?" I asked.

I thought back to the torn document I saw at the funeral. It was definitely typed.

"You could pay a high-priced attorney thousands of dollars to write a will, and it could be trumped by someone later writing a new will out with a ballpoint pen and a piece of paper. If everything was written out correctly, they could even write it on a napkin."

"What are some of the reasons someone might claim a will is invalid then?" I asked.

"They could claim the signature was forged. They could say the testator was unduly influenced or not of sound mind."

"How would you prove that?" I asked.

"A doctor's testimony could do it. Let's say the person was proven to have been suffering from some mental ailment, like Alzheimer's, and there was medical proof of this diagnosis. That could invalidate the will."

"What if I decide to leave everything to my roommate, Foxx, and Alana says that wasn't my intention? How would she go about getting my will declared invalid?" I asked.

"When a will is admitted to probate, the interested parties are all given notice and a hearing is set. If Alana opposed the will, she would need to file notice to prevent the will from being admitted into probate. Once it's admitted, though, the will is essentially proven to be valid. I can't tell you how many times I've heard about family members threatening to contest a will, but if everything was done properly, they really don't have a leg to stand on. Their attorneys tell them that, and they end up not contesting the will after all. It's not worth paying an attorney a lot of money when they don't stand a chance of getting what they want."

"Okay, if the will is valid and no one contests it, how long does it take for things like money and property to be transferred to the new owners?"

"In Hawaii probate could last a minimum of six months. It could also last years or even decades if the interested parties oppose it."

"What happens if Foxx, Alana, and I had a business? Does the business have to stop functioning while the estate is in probate?" I asked.

"Well, if it was a large business, it would be highly unlikely that you were the sole owner. Most likely the company would be structured as an LLC or a corporation. There would be an operating agreement for that entity that would clearly state how things are to be run in the event a general partner dies. For example, if the three of you owned the company, and you left your shares to a fourth person, that person would inherit your interest in the company, but it's not like they can show up at the headquarters one day and expect to vote on how things are done. The operating agreement would prevent that from happening."

"So if Joe inherits his mother's hotel, it's not like he can immediately sell it and pocket the money," I said.

"I thought we established I couldn't talk about my clients," Mara said.

"I had to try. By the way, have you heard of a lawyer named Dick Halverson?"

"No. Why do you ask?"

"He's supposedly the guy who rewrote Charlotte's will."

"I'll ask around. Maybe some of my colleagues know him."

"Give me a call if you learn anything important."

I ended the call. I found it unlikely Mill and Bethany could prove their mother was unduly influenced or wasn't of sound mind. She seemed very coherent to me. Of course, there was always the chance she had a medical condition she didn't disclose to me or Mara. It would have been none of our business.

As far as I knew, that meant Mill and Bethany's best hope of declaring the will invalid was if their mother's signature was forged. I assumed they'd need to bring in a handwriting expert to do that. It wasn't looking good for them.

If I were a betting man, I'd put my money on Joe Chambers to inherit the crown and become a rich man once that hotel property was sold. How long he would manage to hold onto that money was an entirely different scenario. I still didn't know why Charlotte left everything to Joe and excluded her two other children. And why in the world would she agree to use a different lawyer like Dick Halverson to draw up the new will?

When Maui the dog and I got back to the house, Foxx was home.

"Hey, buddy, how's the investigation going?" he asked.

I told him about my morning meeting with Candi, my strange conversation with her lawyer in an empty room, and the lesson in wills from Mara Winters.

"This girl, Candi, actually thought you were there for sex?" Foxx asked.

"Yeah, you should have seen how she was dressed."

"Tempted?"

"Not in the least. I can honestly say I've never hired a prostitute before."

Foxx said nothing.

"You have no follow-up?" I asked.

"Oh, nope, I haven't used one either. I was just thinking about this one girl I was with a few times in college. I'm pretty sure she was running some kind of escort business on the side, but she never charged me."

"Why'd you think she might have been an escort then?" I asked.

"Just some things some other guys said. Doesn't matter. So what are you gonna do now?"

"Depends on what Alana wants to do."

"I think the answer is obvious. The other brother did it. The guy I walked in on doing coke in the bathroom," Fox said.

"Joe Chambers."

"That's the one."

"What makes you think he did it?" I asked.

"Drugs, man. They screw you up big time. The guy sounds like a desperate dude to me. Why would he go to a lawyer like that if something shady wasn't going on? Think about it. His two witnesses for the will are a lawyer with no office furniture and a hooker."

I would have laughed if someone hadn't been murdered. Foxx was right, though. Joe was guilty of something. Maybe it was just royally screwing his life up. Maybe it was a fake will. Maybe it was murder.

"What have you been up to lately? We really haven't had much time to talk in the last week," I said.

"Nothing much. Just taking it easy."

"You been hanging out at Harry's?"

"No more than usual," Foxx said.

"You been dating anyone new?" I asked.

"Why are you so interested in my love life?"

"Sorry, I'm not trying to be nosy. It's just that I find hearing about your love life to be a huge stress reliever for me. It's a bit of a break to hear the stories."

"My fault, man. I hope it didn't sound like I was snapping at you. Nothing's going on in that department. I sometimes feel like people judge me for not being more committed to someone."

"Some people might, not me."

"I appreciate it. I've just decided to take a bit of a break," he said.

I didn't want to press anymore, especially after claiming I held no judgments on the matter, but I knew Foxx wasn't being entirely honest with me. I'd known Foxx for a very long time, and not once in that time have I ever known him to take a break.

"You want a beer?" I asked.

"Sure."

I walked into the kitchen and pulled two beers out of the refrigerator. I went back into the living room and handed Foxx his bottle.

"Thanks."

He twisted the top off and took a big slug.

"Let me ask you a question. How do you know when the time is right to propose to someone?" I asked.

"You thinking about popping the question?"

"The thought crossed my mind. I know we haven't really been together that long, though."

"Has she dropped any hints?" Foxx asked.

"Not at all."

"Then why propose?"

"I don't know. It just seems like the right thing to do."

"I'm not saying it's the right or the wrong thing. It just seems like you two have something pretty good going on. I don't think marriage would ruin that, but why change the status of something if it's going fine?"

It was a good point. Perhaps that would be the same reasoning Alana would use if I did ask her to marry me. Why screw up a good thing?

"Aren't you sort of telling the world you've made a commitment to each other?" I asked.

"Yeah, but who cares what the world thinks? Marriage started out as more of a legal contract. It was all about money and inheriting land. What does she have to offer you? Have you had a look at her dowry?"

Foxx paused a moment, and then he laughed. "Whatever happened to dowries? We desperately need to get back to that," he said.

"What about you? You ever see yourself getting married?" I asked.

"I thought about it once, but you already know that."

Foxx was referring to his girlfriend, Lauren. He'd admitted that he'd seriously considered proposing to her before she was murdered.

"I did. I guess I was just thinking more long-term. Is it something you see yourself doing sometime in the future?" I asked.

Foxx took another long pull from his beer. Then he put the empty bottle down on the table.

"Nope. I honestly can't see that happening."

Alana came by a couple of hours later. We sat by the pool and watched the sunset. I told her about Foxx's theory on Joe Chambers being the guilty party. She said all of those thoughts had crossed her mind, too, especially after I phoned her about my conversations with Candi and Dick Halverson.

"Does that mean you want to interview Joe again in the morning?" I asked.

"Actually, I'd rather start with Mill and Bethany. I want to hear their take on all this. I think there's more going on than Joe's drug habit."

I understood exactly what Alana was saying. There was a part of me that thought Joe was too obvious. It couldn't be that easy, could it? A guy desperate for money to fuel his drug and alcohol problems murders his mother and forges a will to guarantee he gets her estate. On the other hand, I did have a habit of overthinking things. Maybe I was looking for a complex answer when the problem was two plus two equals Joe did it. I thought about Occam's razor – the simplest explanation tends to be the correct one. I decided to give my brain a break and radically changed the subject.

"Not that Maui isn't an awesome place...but we should go somewhere when this is all over," I said.

"Where do you want to go?"

"I didn't have a specific place in mind. Just somewhere else. You said you never traveled much. Let's change that."

"Okay, I'll start thinking of places."

"Pick any place, any place at all," I said.

"And who's paying for this trip?"

I looked back to the house.

"We'll get Foxx to pay for it. He's got the money."

9

JEN CHAMBERS

ALANA DIDN'T SPEND THE NIGHT AT FOXX'S, SO I DROVE OVER TO HER house early the next morning. She invited me inside and led me back into her kitchen.

"You want anything to eat or drink?" she asked.

"Just a glass of water, but I'll get it."

I walked over to one of the cabinets and removed a tall glass. I filled it under the faucet.

"You don't want some of the cold water in the fridge?" she asked.

"Actually, I'm more of a room-temperature guy."

Alana made herself a cup of coffee, and we sat outside on her patio.

"Who do we interview first? Mill or Bethany?" Alana asked.

"I say Jen."

"Jen? Mill's wife?"

"We know Mrs. Chambers didn't like her based on the comment she made in the notes to me. Maybe the feeling was mutual."

"And you're guessing she might be more forthcoming."

"At least she might give us a different perspective on the Chambers family dynamic," I said.

"If Mill is the guilty party, do you think he brought Jen in on it?" Alana asked.

"I don't know, but judging by the close relationship they showed at the party, I bet she at least suspects something is up, if he's guilty, that is."

Alana and I drove to Mill and Jen Chambers' house. They lived in Kihei, not far from Joe Chambers. The neighborhood was about the same as Joe's. In fact, the house was also about the same size, which was a bit surprising considering Mill and Jen had a family of four, and Joe was by himself. Of course, they might have downsized once their kids left for college. There was also the fact Maui was a very expensive place to live. You were bound to be in a small house unless you had big bucks.

We parked on the street and climbed out of the car. There was a blue Ford Explorer parked in the driveway. It was a considerable notch below the Mercedes I saw at Joe's house. I wasn't sure if this meant Mill and Jen were more conservative with their money or if Charlotte Chambers had been feeding Joe a lot more cash. We rang the doorbell, and Jen answered.

"Good morning, Jen," I said.

"Mill's already left for work. If you need to talk to him, your best bet would be to go to the hotel," she said.

"Actually, we wanted to speak with you. Do you mind if we come in and ask you a few questions?" Alana asked.

Jen looked surprised, and I wondered if the lady had spent most of her life living in the shadow of Mill Chambers. I found the thought depressing.

"No problem," she said.

We walked inside and Jen led us to a lanai at the back of the house.

"Can I get you anything to drink?" she asked.

"No, thank you. I'm fine," Alana said.

"I'm fine too," I said.

We sat on a comfortable sofa that allowed us a good look at the backyard. It might have been better described as an oasis. Large palm trees, colorful flowers, and thick tropical plants were everywhere. Everything looked beautiful and well cared for. Jen sat in a matching chair directly across from us.

"What a gorgeous yard," Alana said.

Jen smiled.

"Do you maintain this all yourself?" I asked.

"Yes. It started out as a little side project when the kids went off to school. Then I just kept expanding it over the years. I'm afraid it's a little out of control at the moment."

"I wouldn't change a thing. It's spectacular," I said.

"You really think so?" Jen asked.

"I agree with Poe. It's perfect," Alana said.

"You obviously have a gift for this. Have you thought about doing something like this at the Chambers Hotel?" I asked.

Jen's smile vanished.

"I've made the offer a few times. They're not interested."

"Who's not interested? Mill?"

"No, Mill's all for it. Charlotte wasn't," Jen said.

"How is Mill? I know he's been through a lot this week," I said.

"He's holding up. Mill's a lot stronger than people give him credit for."

I wasn't sure what people she was referring to or why they might not think Mill was strong.

"What questions did you want to ask me?"

"Jen, did you know that Charlotte suspected one of her children wanted to kill her because she received threatening letters?" Alana asked.

Alana's timing was impeccable, and her delivery was smooth and without emotion. We had debated on the way over whether to drop that little bomb on Jen. Ultimately, we decided it was the right move since it would undoubtedly throw her off balance. That was always the condition we wanted people to be in during interviews. Furthermore, Jen might be willing to spill family secrets in an effort to deflect suspicion from Mill and put the attention on Bethany and Joe. Judging by the look of shock we got, I'd say we succeeded.

"She actually told you that?" Jen asked.

"I was hired by Mrs. Chambers through her attorney Mara Winters. She came to Ms. Winters after getting the second letter. That's why she threw the birthday party for her late husband. It was a chance for me to interact with the family."

"Then a third note appeared that night, which is when we hired the security team," Alana said.

"Only Mrs. Chambers dismissed the team in the morning and pulled a vanishing act," I said.

"That doesn't surprise me. Charlotte didn't like anyone telling her what to do." Jen shook her head. "I can't believe she actually thought one of her own children would be behind this, the nerve of that woman."

I'd kept my eyes on Jen's the entire conversation. Only an accomplished liar could prevent the truth from showing up in his or her eyes. I sensed she'd been telling the truth so far, and I saw her emotions change from confusion to bewilderment to anger. I wasn't sure if she was angry at Alana and me or Mrs. Chambers. It was probably a little of both. I didn't blame her if she was innocent. That's one of the problems with these investigations. You end up potentially accusing a lot of innocent people of doing really bad things.

"That's why you're here?" Jen continued. "You think Mill had something to do with her death? You think he drowned his own mother in that pool?"

"That's not it at all, and I apologize if we gave you that impression. We're trying to get a better understanding of Mrs. Chambers and who may have wanted to hurt her. The family knew her better than anyone," Alana said.

I didn't think Jen believed her, but she didn't immediately accuse Alana of lying to her, nor did she demand we leave the house. She just sat there, staring at the floor. I assumed she was asking herself how much she should tell us.

She looked up at us, and all I saw in her eyes was sorrow.

"Mill loved her despite all the garbage she put him through," Jen said.

"What would she do to him?" I asked.

"She never made him feel like he was good enough. He could never live up to the Millard Chambers name."

"Was his father hard on him, too?" I asked.

"Mill started at the bottom of that hotel. His father had him cleaning rooms, vacuuming the pool, and doing the landscaping. People assume Mill just stepped into the manager's role, but he worked his tail off for it. And you know what he got? He's paid a good 10 percent less than other managers on the island. Can you believe that? His own mother paid him less than the competition would."

"Did he ever think of going somewhere else?" I asked.

"I begged him to, but he would never consider it. He said the hotel would be his one day. I never believed it."

"Why's that?" Alana asked.

"Joe was always the favorite. He could do no wrong in Charlotte's eyes, but the guy's a train wreck. It still didn't surprise me, though, that she'd leave him everything."

"What about Mill? Did it surprise him?" I asked.

"He's heartbroken. He still doesn't believe it."

"And Bethany? How did she take it?" Alana asked.

"I didn't speak with her or Barry. Mill did. He said it was bad."

"I'm sorry to bring this up," I said, "but Mrs. Chambers gave me the impression that you two didn't get along."

Jen laughed. "She did, did she?"

"Can we take that as confirmation that you two weren't exactly best friends?" Alana asked.

"She hated me from the first moment she laid eyes on me, but I was never anything but nice to her."

"What do you think it was then?" I asked.

"At first I thought it was just a mother and her son thing. Some mothers don't think anyone is good enough for their son, but I eventually came to believe something else. Charlotte could be a very cruel person when she wanted to be."

The statement floored me. I'd gotten no indications of that during my interactions with Mrs. Chambers, brief as they were. Was she entirely innocent? I didn't know anymore.

"She accused me on more than one occasion of being after Mill's money, which was a joke. He didn't have a penny to his name when I met him. People assume we have a lot of money because Mill's family owns a successful hotel, but all Mill gets is his manager's salary. Charlotte kept all the company's profits for herself."

That stunned me, and it made me realize just how deeply cut Mill and Jen must have been when the new will emerged. They'd spent a lifetime at that hotel and now had nothing to show for it.

"I know Mill is the general manager and Bethany and Barry run the marketing department," Alana said.

"If you can call it that. The only reason those two have a job is because they're family members. Barry doesn't even show up for work half the time. He practically lives on the golf course."

This was coming from a woman who Mrs. Chambers claimed had never worked a day in her life, but was that true? Again, I didn't know. I was now questioning everything Mrs. Chambers told me.

"What does Joe do at the hotel?" I asked.

"He manages the bar, at least that's what he tells people. Mill oversees most of those responsibilities, though. Joe really just bartends at night. He drinks half the inventory himself."

I thought about Joe's Mercedes. I doubted he'd make the kind of tips at the Chambers Hotel that he'd need to buy a vehicle like that. When I made my short walk around the hotel pool, I saw mostly families with young kids. They're notoriously bad tippers, so Joe was either the highest paid bartender on the island or Mama Chambers was slipping him serious bucks on the side. It looked like Joe was the favored child after all, but I knew that already after having seen the new will. Furthermore, Mill and Bethany would have had to come to the same conclusion about their mother sharing some, or a lot of, the profits with Joe and not them. It had to have really gotten under their skin. I didn't know if that was enough reason in one of their minds to commit murder, especially of their own mother.

"Mrs. Chambers said she'd recently received an offer to sell the hotel. Did you know anything about that?" Alana asked.

"Marriott offered to buy it. They have several timeshares on the island. I think they wanted to tear down the hotel and build more of those."

"Was Mill in favor of selling?" I asked.

"No, he wanted her to keep the hotel."

"Was he worried he wouldn't receive any of the proceeds? You just said Mrs. Chambers never shared out the profits," Alana said.

"That wasn't it. Mill loves his job. He's never missed a day of work. He goes in early every day and stays late. He loves the people he meets. It's his dream job. He wouldn't know what to do with himself if he wasn't there anymore."

"Do you know if Mrs. Chambers knew he felt that way?" I asked.

"I don't see how she couldn't. He didn't have any reason to hide that from her."

"What about Bethany and Joe? Did they want her to sell?" Alana asked.

"Absolutely. They both pushed her to. They even came to Mill and tried to get him on their side, but he refused."

"Were they upset enough to try to scare her with those letters?" I asked.

"Certainly not enough to kill her," Jen said.

"Who would want to kill her? You said she could be cruel. Who are we not looking at?" Alana asked.

"Mill said there was a man who came to him after news got out about the potential deal with Marriott. The man said his father used to be Millard Senior's business partner."

"A partner in the hotel?" I asked.

Jen nodded. "Mill said his father actually bought the property with help from his partner. They built the hotel together. They had a falling out of some kind, and Millard Senior bought him out. Mill said the partner's son came to him and demanded half the money from the sale of the property. Mill had never even met the guy before, and he told him to leave."

"What was his name?" Alana asked.

"I don't know his first name, but the last name is Edelman. I didn't even know Millard had a partner until this incident. Charlotte made it seem like her husband did everything on his own."

"Did Mill say whether this Edelman guy ever visited Mrs. Chambers?" I asked.

"He never said anything about it. I can ask, though."

"Please do," Alana said.

Alana turned to me. "Anything else?"

I shook my head, and Alana turned back to Jen.

"You've been a tremendous help. Thank you," Alana said.

"You should go to the hotel if you want to speak with Mill. He has nothing to hide. He'll tell you anything you want to know."

Alana and I thanked her again and walked back to the car. Alana started the engine and cranked up the air conditioner.

"She was pretty forthcoming. You think she was playing us?" Alana asked.

"Maybe. But I doubt it. She couldn't stand Charlotte. It was probably fantastic for her to have us as a captive audience so she could really unload on the lady. Who else was she going to talk to other than us and Mill, and I'm sure he's sick of hearing her tell him how lousy his mother was. It's not like he can do anything about it since he worked for the lady and their livelihood depended on him staying on her good side."

"I can't even imagine what that must have been like for him, and especially Jen. It must have been hard being reliant on a woman who you know doesn't like you," Alana said.

Alana put the car in drive and pulled away from the curb.

"Do we go see this Edelman? It shouldn't be hard to find out who Millard's partner was, and how many Edelmans can there be on this island?" I asked.

"You just read my mind."

10

TREVOR EDELMAN

As it turned out, there was only one Edelman on the island. His name was Trevor Edelman, and he owned a small boat-building business in Lahaina. It wasn't hard to find the tiny warehouse that housed his company. The structure looked fairly worn out. The white paint was faded and peeling in numerous places. The parking lot was covered with deep potholes. There really wasn't a path you could navigate to avoid hitting at least a few of them on your way in and out. Alana parked the car near the entrance to the warehouse. It didn't appear to have an office attached to it. It was really just a large metal box.

We heard rock music blaring through the open warehouse door the moment we climbed out of the car. It wasn't hard to mistake the sounds of Pink Floyd.

"Looks like this place got bombed out," I said as we walked across the parking lot.

I looked up at a small wooden sign that hung over the open doorway. "Edelman Designs" was written in pale letters across a faded-pink background that probably had been red when it was first painted.

Alana and I entered the warehouse and spotted a few employees working on various wooden canoes. The gorgeous watercrafts were all in different stages of completion. Most of them looked like they were based on ancient Hawaiian designs. They had a typical canoe-like structure in the middle, but many of them also had wooden attachments on either one or both sides. I assumed this was for better balance in the high waves of the ocean. I wasn't sure who Trevor Edelman's customer base was, maybe hotels or clubs that wanted these things for ceremonial purposes or decoration. They were hand-made - at least I didn't see any large machines in the warehouse. The wood looked of superior quality, so I imagined these things cost a pretty penny.

We approached the first employee we came across and asked for Trevor. The man pointed to a fifty-year-old near the back of the warehouse. He was of average height and was muscular, probably from cutting and sanding boats every day. We walked over to him. He ignored us as he chiseled away at a block of wood.

"Trevor Edelman?" Alana asked.

"Who wants to know?" Trevor asked. He looked up at Alana and smiled, which made the statement come across as more friendly than hostile.

"I'm Detective Alana Hu, and this is my associate, Mr. Rutherford."

"In that case, I'm not Edelman," he said, and he smiled again.

"All jokes aside, is there somewhere we can go to speak in private?" Alana asked

"Sure."

Trevor put down the chisel and led us out a back door. We walked over to a picnic table that had been placed under a large tree. I admired the beautifully constructed table while the three of us sat.

"Is this handmade too?" I asked.

"Yeah, it turned out well, I think."

"Beautiful," I said, as I ran my hand across the smooth surface.

"I was wondering if I was going to get a visit from the police," he said.

"And why is that?" Alana asked.

"My guess is Chambers told you about our little conversation."

"He described it as more of an argument," Alana said.

"Maybe that's the way he saw it."

"How would you describe it?" Alana asked.

"Like I said before, it was a conversation."

"I'm sure you heard about the death of Charlotte Chambers," Alana said.

"On the news. It was a terrible thing. I always liked her."

"Mill made it sound like you didn't like any member of the Chambers family," I said.

"Mostly that's true, but Charlotte was different."

"How so?" Alana asked.

"She lacked the Chambers arrogance, at least around me," Trevor said.

"You saw her frequently?" I asked.

"Not really. Maybe once a year or so. We would mainly just bump into each other from time to time."

"Were those encounters awkward?" Alana asked.

"Why should they be?" he asked.

"Seems like your family and theirs had a falling out. I would think that would make things a bit strained when you saw each other."

"My issue was more with her husband and her kids."

"Why is that?"

"As I said before, the arrogance. It's my least favorite of the personality traits."

"You say Millard Chambers was an arrogant man. Everyone I've talked to described him as a great guy," I said.

"And who is everyone? His kids? I'm guessing you never met him. Maybe *arrogant* isn't the best word to describe him. Perhaps *world-class asshole* would be more appropriate," Trevor said.

That's three words, but who's counting, I thought.

"Mill Chambers said you demanded a portion of the proceeds from the sale of the hotel. How did you hear about the potential sale?" Alana asked.

"I ran into the youngest one, Joe, at a bar. He was drunk, and when he saw me, he came over to gloat about the sale of the hotel. He said it was going to go for tens of millions."

"Your father was once one of the owners of the hotel. Is that right?" I asked.

"Chambers and my father had known each other since childhood. They had been best friends. He asked my father to go into business with him. He found the property for the hotel, but my father provided the connections for the funding."

I didn't know what "connections for the funding" meant. Did that mean he knew the guy at the bank, or was there under-the-table money involved?

"Why did they eventually part ways?" Alana asked.

"The way my father described it was they had very different visions for the company. That translated to constant arguments. My father offered to buy him out, but he refused."

"So your father accepted a buyout from Millard?" I asked.

"If you can call it that. It was a ridiculously low offer. My father refused at first, but Chambers made his life a living hell. He ended up accepting it just to get away from him."

"Did your father ever consider opening a new hotel by himself?" I asked.

"He told me he did, but he ultimately decided to go into other business areas."

Judging by the dilapidated setting of Edelman Designs, I guessed they hadn't worked out. Either that or he left money to Trevor that was promptly blown on expensive cars and frivolous possessions.

"You know you have no legal claim to that hotel," I said.

Trevor's mood immediately darkened.

"Let me ask you something. How would you feel if that jackass Joe Chambers approached you in a bar and said what he said? You think that idiot deserves that money? What did he ever do?"

"He is Millard Chambers' son," I said.

Trevor looked away. I thought he might stand at that moment and leave us sitting there under the tree, but he turned back.

"Chambers screwed my family out of millions. His kids need to make that right."

"How do they do that? Give you half the money?" Alana asked.

Trevor said nothing.

"Where were you the night Charlotte Chambers was killed?" Alana asked.

"Now we really get to why you're here. Did one of her kids accuse me of doing it?" he asked.

"No one has accused you of anything," Alana said.

"I was at the warehouse all day. My employees can vouch for me. Afterward, I went into town for dinner. Then I came back here to work again."

"I don't suppose there was anyone with you that night," Alana said.

"No, I was alone."

There was a long pause in the conversation before Trevor spoke again.

"Two things - if I did kill Charlotte Chambers, don't you think I would have tried to come up with a better story than I was alone at work?"

"And the second thing?" Alana asked.

"What did I have to gain by killing the lady? I still don't have any part of that hotel or their money. You're looking in the wrong place," Trevor said.

"Where should we be looking?" I asked.

"Try the family. They can all rot in hell for all I care."

"Does that include Charlotte?" I asked.

"She didn't deserve what she got," Trevor said.

"You've really thought this through, haven't you? You have an answer for everything," Alana said.

"I'm innocent. Why wouldn't I have an answer for everything?"

Trevor studied both Alana and me for a response. We didn't give him one.

"Is there anything else?" Trevor asked.

"No," Alana said.

Trevor stood and walked back to the warehouse. Alana and I stayed at the picnic table.

"What does your gut tell you?" she asked.

"He didn't do it."

"Did you sense he was holding anything back?"

"Not really. My guess is he grew irate when a drunk Joe Chambers rubbed the money in his face. I can't blame him for that. I would be angry too. His visit to Mill Chambers was probably more to let off steam than anything else. Maybe he thought the family would give him money to avoid a lawsuit."

"Did Mara mention a lawsuit to you?" Alana asked.

"No, but I'm sure the Chambers family may be thinking one is coming. You know people can sue for any reason these days. Lawyers recommend settling a lot of the time because it's way cheaper than going through the actual court proceedings, even if you know you're going to win."

"You think so?" Alana asked.

"Absolutely. I have a friend I went to school with who's now a lawyer in Atlanta. He represents a lot of companies who get sued for sexual harassment. Most of the time the male executives are actually innocent, but the companies settle anyway. It's a huge racket, and a lot of lawyers make good money just filing frivolous lawsuits."

"Let's say he intends to shake the family down for money. That reinforces his argument that he had nothing to gain by killing Charlotte."

"That's true, but there's always the revenge factor. His line about only admiring Charlotte seemed a bit of a stretch to me."

I looked down at the table.

"This is a hell of a piece of work. I was half tempted to ask him how much he'd charge to make another one," I said.

"That would have come out well. We think you might have killed Charlotte Chambers, but let's talk woodworking first."

"Good point. Did you see how many guys he's got working in there?" I asked.

"I think I saw three."

"That's how many I saw. There were way more boats than guys. Either a bunch of people called in sick today, or his business isn't doing so well and he can't afford more people."

"The boats looked beautiful, but I can't imagine there are many people in the market for an old-style Hawaiian outrigger," Alana said.

"I was thinking the same thing while we were in there. The guy's got real talent for something but maybe not much demand for it. I bet if you looked into his finances you'd discover he's in deep debt. Maybe he did go to Charlotte after his argument with Mill and demand money from her. Maybe he thought he could scare her more easily."

"Let's say he did that. Why would Charlotte change the will at that point? He's got nothing to do with her kids. As weird as it sounds, maybe she would even be somewhat relieved knowing it was someone other than a family member who had threatened her."

"Everything keeps coming back to the will, doesn't it?" I asked.

"Do you have the energy for one more interview today?"

"You thinking Bethany and Barry?"

Alana nodded.

11

BETHANY AND BARRY WILLIAMS

WE LEFT TREVOR EDELMAN'S AND WENT STRAIGHT TO SEE BETHANY and Barry. They lived in Wailea, not far from Charlotte's house. Their quaint home was at the end of a narrow road that ran through the center of their neighborhood. The grass looked freshly cut, and the bushes in front of the house were neatly trimmed. You could tell they cared for their property.

Barry answered the door and led us into the living room, which was in the back. We saw Bethany sitting in a chair by the window. She didn't rise to greet us, which I found rather odd. I wasn't sure if she was attempting to pull a power play of some kind.

"May I get you anything?" Barry asked us.

"No, I'm good," Alana said.

"I'm fine, too. Thanks," I said.

"Please have a seat," Barry said, and he sat down in a chair near Bethany's.

Alana and I sat on a sofa across from them. It was rather stiff and uncomfortable. I looked around the room. It didn't seem very lived in, and I wondered if they treated this as one of those old-style living rooms that people only used when they had guests. I always found that arrangement a colossal waste of square footage.

"How's the investigation coming?" Bethany asked.

"We just had a conversation with Trevor Edelman. Do you know him?" Alana asked.

"Of course, but I haven't seen him in years."

"Your brother, Mill, said Trevor came to see him a short while ago and demanded a share of the potential sale of the company," Alana said.

"Really?" Bethany said.

"Mill didn't say anything to you?" I asked.

"No, but we usually only talk about the hotel operations."

"Surely this would fall under that category," Alana said.

"I don't see how. Trevor has no claim at all to our hotel. His father signed away his ownership years ago."

"Has he made similar claims before now?" I asked.

"Not that I know of. Like I said before, I haven't seen him in a long time. I don't even remember the last time I saw him."

"Did your mother say anything about him?" Alana asked. "Did he make any threats to her?"

"No. Nothing," Bethany said.

"Do you think he has something to do with Charlotte's murder?" Barry asked.

"We're not sure. That's one of the reasons we wanted to talk to you," I said.

"You told me a few days ago that you couldn't think of anyone who would want to harm your mother. Is that still the case?" Alana asked.

"I wish I could give you a name. I'd love to give you a name, but I just don't know of anyone," Bethany said.

"Before your mother passed, how were things at the hotel?" I asked.

"What do you mean?" Bethany asked.

"Was business good? Were there any disagreements over the operations?"

"No, everything was fine. It's a tough job, and the work can be extremely demanding, but what job isn't these days?"

"You and Barry do the marketing for the hotel, right?" Alana asked.

Bethany nodded.

"Do you find the work fulfilling?" Alana asked.

"It's not that it's fulfilling or not fulfilling. It's a means to an end."

"And what is that?" I asked.

"Providing for our family," Barry said.

"Jen mentioned to us that Mrs. Chambers didn't share the profits from the hotel. Is that correct?" Alana asked.

I studied Bethany closely, assuming her reaction might display the truth of her feelings toward her late mother, but she had no reaction. There wasn't even a fake smile. Her expression was about as neutral as you could get. It was so weird to me. Her mother had been murdered, and she didn't seem the least bothered by it. I know that's me judging someone, and we all handle stress and pain differently, but shouldn't she be showing some form of emotion or realness, if that's even a word?

Her answers to Alana's questions were coming off to me as measured, rehearsed, and anything but authentic. It was like we were an employer, and she was interviewing for a job.

"What is your biggest weakness, Bethany?"

"Well, I'm a perfectionist, and I work too hard."

Back in reality, Bethany said, "I'm not sure what our finances have to do with this investigation."

"They have everything to do with it," Alana said. She then informed the couple of the origins of my involvement, including a vague description of my first conversation with Charlotte Chambers and Mara Winters. Of course, she left out the part about Charlotte thinking one of her adult kids was responsible for the drugged pinot.

Again, Bethany's reaction was blank. I wasn't sure if the woman was a robot, if she was hiding something, or if she had already been informed about the nature of my investigation by her sister-in-law, Jen. Maybe it was all of the above.

"Did you want your mother to sell the hotel?" I asked.

"Of course. The property was worth way more than the hotel

business itself. The offer my mother received was more than generous. She planned to take it," Bethany said.

"That surprises me. When I met with your mother, she told me she'd never sell," I said.

"I don't know why she would say that," Bethany said.

"Something to do with a promise she made to your father to never sell the business."

Bethany laughed.

"She was still telling that old story," Bethany said.

"Charlotte was a smart business woman. She knew the longer she held out, the higher their offer would go. That's all," Barry said.

"What you're saying is that Mrs. Chambers intended to sell the hotel after all?" Alana asked.

"Absolutely. She told us that numerous times, but it wasn't just the money. It was also about the family," Bethany said.

"I don't understand," Alana said.

"My mother knew we weren't going to be able to run the business after she was gone. Mill and I can't agree on anything. And Joe, he's just hopeless."

"Your mother was going to sell the property to keep her children from tearing each other apart?" I asked.

Bethany nodded.

"Did Mill know your mother was going to sell? We were under the impression he wanted her to keep the business," I said.

"He probably wanted her to sell more than we did. He couldn't wait to get out of that place," Bethany said.

"Jen told us Mill lives for that job," Alana said.

"Mill spends the entire day looking at his watch. He can't wait for the night manager to arrive," Bethany said.

"What does Jen have to gain, though, by telling us Mill loves the hotel business?" I asked.

"Well, Jen's not exactly the most honest person," Barry said, and then he chuckled. It was one of those things people sometimes do when they've just criticized someone, sort of like using the phrase "bless his heart" after a royal slam.

"Why do you say that?" I asked.

"Because she lies constantly, even when telling the truth would benefit her. I've never seen anything like it, but she's always been like that. It's just something we've gotten used to," Barry said.

It was obvious what this couple was doing. Bethany played the good cop, and Barry was the one who went on the attack. I wasn't sure if this was their normal way of doing things or if they had prepared a plan for how to deal with Alana and me. I thought about their coworkers at the hotel. Could you imagine working with this pair? I think I'd last all of two days.

"Is there something you think Jen is trying to keep us from learning?" I asked.

"I don't have the slightest idea. I'm just saying she's not being honest if she told you Mill didn't want his mother to sell the hotel. He hates that job, and he's bitter toward his mother for not giving him more money. I'm guessing Jen also told you how Mill makes less than other managers on the island," Barry said.

"Is that true?" I asked.

"I don't know if it's true, and that's the point. There's no way for Jen or Mill to know either, unless they personally called every manager and asked them what they made. It's just a common complaint they have. I don't think a week goes by without them telling us how underappreciated Mill is," Barry said.

"I imagine that can happen in family businesses. Did you two feel you were appreciated?" Alana asked.

"My mother never went around dishing out compliments, but that's just the way she was. I knew she valued Barry and me. Mill knows she valued him, too, and if he doesn't, then he just doesn't have a good grasp on reality," Bethany said.

"How did Mill take it when he found out about the new will?" Alana asked.

"He was furious, of course," Bethany said, "but he knows it's a fake."

"Why do you think that?" I asked.

"My mother would never leave everything to Joe. She told me just a month ago that she was thinking of leaving him out completely."

"Why would she do that?" Alana asked.

"The drugs. She knew he wasn't clean, despite what she might have said to others. She didn't want him to have a generous supply of money to fuel his habit."

"Do you think Joe forged the will?" Alana asked.

"Absolutely. Does it make any sense to you that my mother would suddenly change her will and leave everything to a drug addict? Do you really think she would trust the business to him after all my father did to build it? And what about Mill and me? Why would she leave us out?"

The thought crossed my mind to inform Bethany that her mother had described her children to me as greedy bastards. Still, Bethany did bring up a good point. It made no sense to me that Charlotte would leave Joe everything. She didn't give me the impression that she was a woman who kept her head in the sand. She had to have known Joe was still using, and there would have been no reason for Joe to stop once he got his hands on the Chambers fortune.

"I know what you're thinking, Detective," Bethany said.

"And what is that?" Alana asked.

"You think someone in the family is responsible for my mother's death."

"Why would I think that?"

"We had the most to gain, obviously, but neither Barry nor I did it. We were working at the hotel all day. There are over a dozen employees who can vouch for us. Afterward, we had dinner with our daughter here at the house. I can't speak for the whereabouts of Mill or Joe, but I know my brothers. We don't agree on much, but I know neither of them would ever raise a hand to our mother, let alone drown her in a pool. The thought is preposterous."

"Who did kill her then?" Alana asked.

"I've been asking myself that non-stop, and I keep coming up empty," Bethany said.

There really wasn't anywhere to go after that little monologue.

Alana thanked them for their time, and we walked out to her car. She started the engine and drove away, but she pulled over after driving a few blocks.

"Bethany paints her brother as hating his job and desperate for his mother to sell the hotel, whereas Jen says her husband is a dream employee," Alana said.

"I've seldom met a dream employee, especially one who felt he was chronically underpaid, but we shouldn't be surprised that Jen wanted to make her husband look like a saint," I said.

"And what about Barry's comment that Jen is a compulsive liar?" Alana asked.

"Again, I'm not surprised. We kind of knew the two families didn't get along. Did it strike you as a bit convenient that they had dinner with their daughter the night Charlotte was killed?"

"It's certainly not unusual for families to dine together, but it does seem ironic that the entire Williams clan can alibi each other. What are the odds the two families are in this together?" Alana asked.

"Why give different stories then? Almost everything they said contradicts the other."

"Exactly. It creates more doubt. Wouldn't it seem rather odd to us if their stories perfectly matched? That's what would really create suspicion," Alana said.

"Okay, let's assume you're right, and Mill and Bethany both planned the murder. Are Jen and Barry also in on it? Who did the deed? That's a lot of people to trust and an awful lot of risk. What about how they all feel about each other? I don't think they're faking those bad feelings."

"Greed makes for strange bedfellows. Isn't that a saying?" Alana asked.

"I'm not sure, but it should be if it isn't."

"Have we reached the point where we're starting to throw out crazy theories because we don't know where else to turn?" Alana asked.

"Maybe. Probably," I said.

"What are the other theories?"

I wanted to say something insightful and brilliant, but I had nothing. I was more confused now than ever before.

"Do you believe the new will is legit?" I asked.

"Mara seems to think Charlotte's signatures are identical," Alana said.

"Why leave out Mill and Jen? What did Charlotte learn that made her change everything, and why risk all her fortune on a guy who clearly can't be trusted with money?" I asked.

"If she learned one of them was behind the threatening notes, why not call the police? And if she didn't want the police involved, why not call you?" Alana asked.

"That's the thing. You just said 'one of them.' She wouldn't have written both of them out of the will if it was just one of them. Maybe your theory isn't so crazy. Maybe she realized they both had something to do with the threatening notes."

"I don't know. The more we talk this out, the more absurd it sounds. I'm not sure those two could actually plan something that complex together," Alana said.

12

SURPRISES

On the way back, Alana and I ended up stopping at the Chambers Hotel to interview Mill. I won't put the dialogue down here because we really didn't learn much.

He confirmed that he'd gotten a visit from Trevor Edelman, who demanded the Chambers family share the proceeds of the potential hotel sale with the Edelman family. Mill said he wasn't worried about it because he knew they didn't have a legal right to anything. He doubted Trevor had spoken to Charlotte since his mother would have undoubtedly said something to him about it. Mill backed up his sister's claim that their mother debated whether to drop Joe from the will since she didn't want to fund his drug habit. He agreed with Bethany that the will was probably fake, and he expressed regret at having gotten into a fight with Joe at the wake. He said he was deeply embarrassed by his actions.

The only mildly new thing we learned was that he mentioned his wife misspoke when she said he didn't want Charlotte to sell the hotel. I love the word "misspoke" because it can be used as an apology or to cover a lie. For example, "I'm sorry I misspoke when I said those jeans make your butt look fat. I meant to say you look fantastic." Mill said he would have been fine if his mother didn't sell because he liked working at the hotel. You'll notice he used the word "like" and not "love."

After the meeting with Mill, Alana and I drove back to her house. It was dark by the time we got there.

"We should watch a movie tonight and maybe order some take-out," Alana said.

"What did you have in mind?"

"Movie or the food?" she asked.

"Food."

"I was thinking Chinese, but now I feel like a burger."

"What do you say we order a couple of burgers from Harry's? I'd like to swing by my place on the way there and pick up the dog. I know Foxx gets tired of watching him. You mind if I bring Maui back here?"

"Not at all," she said.

"Do me a favor and call in the order. I'll see you in about an hour."

I got home in no time and was a little surprised to see a white sedan in Foxx's driveway. If you read *Wedding Day Dead*, you'd know exactly whose car it was. I parked behind the car and went inside. Maui the dog greeted me. I walked into my bedroom and shoved some clothes into a backpack. I already had some toiletries at Alana's.

Then I walked toward the kitchen to grab Maui's water bowl and some of his food. I spotted Hani, Alana's sister, bending over in front of the refrigerator. She was wearing a large T-shirt and nothing else. My guess was the shirt belonged to Foxx.

"Looking for anything in particular?" I asked.

I clearly startled Hani because she did a little jump. She turned to face me.

"Foxx said he thought you were spending the night at Alana's."

"I am. I just came back to get some clothes and my dog."

"I'd appreciate it if you could keep this to yourself."

"Why? What's the big deal?" I asked.

"It's just that I'd rather Alana not know."

"Hey, buddy."

I turned around and saw Foxx standing behind me. Fortunately, he was wearing more than just a T-shirt.

"I thought you were spending the night at Alana's," he said.

"I was or, I am. Can I talk to you in private?" I asked.

"Sure."

Hani grabbed a beer out of the refrigerator and walked back toward Foxx's bedroom.

"I'm on my way out now. Should we talk outside?" I asked.

Foxx nodded, and we both walked out to my car. I picked up Maui and placed him in the passenger seat. I then tossed my backpack and Maui's stuff into the small trunk.

"This has been going on since Charlotte's party, right?" I asked.

"How did you know?"

"I haven't seen you with a girl in over a week. Then you gave me that line about taking a break from women, which I didn't buy for one second."

"It was kind of a weak line, wasn't it?"

"Yeah," I said.

"We hit it off at the party. When I took her home, she asked if I wanted to come inside. I didn't think much about it. We had a few more drinks, several more drinks actually, and one thing led to another..." Foxx said.

"You realize she has a thing about not telling the truth," I said.

"Yeah, you warned me about her, but it's not like I'm about to marry the girl. We're just having a little fun."

"You mean sex," I said.

"Have you seen that girl? You're telling me you wouldn't do exactly what I'm doing if Alana wasn't in the equation?"

I didn't answer his question, but we both already knew the answer.

"Why doesn't Hani want Alana to know?" I asked.

"Beats me, but I didn't say anything to you because she said you'd blab to Alana."

"Hani said that? She used the word *blab*?"

"I think so, but what difference does it make which word she used?" Foxx asked.

"I don't like someone thinking I'm a blabber. I've never been a blabber."

"Are you gonna do it?" Foxx asked.

"Do what?"

"Blab to Alana."

"No, of course not. I'll respect you and Hani's request for secrecy, but if Alana asks me point blank, I'm not going to lie to her."

"Fair enough. But she won't ask. She doesn't know anything," Foxx said.

"Don't be so sure. She's hard to fool," I said.

I told Foxx goodnight and climbed into the car. I turned to the dog.

"How long have you known about this, and why didn't you say anything to me? At least no one accused you of being a blabber," I said, but Maui didn't answer me.

I drove to Harry's and picked up the two burgers along with two huge orders of fries. Alana had changed into a T-shirt and shorts by the time I got back. It was a casual outfit for sure, but she looked fantastic.

We ate dinner while we watched the 1941 Bogart film *The Maltese Falcon*. Alana had never seen it. I had, but it had been so long ago that I remembered very few details.

"I shouldn't have eaten that burger," she said.

"You feeling sick?"

"No, just beyond full."

We decided to watch another Bogart film, *The Big Sleep*, but we both fell asleep on the sofa before we got halfway through. It wasn't boring by any means. I think we were both just exhausted by the long day of interviews. It was after midnight before we stumbled into Alana's bedroom. Maui the dog followed us in there. He likes to sleep under her bed for some strange reason.

I woke up early despite having gone to bed so late. Alana was still asleep. I walked into her living room and heard Maui's footsteps behind me tapping across Alana's wooden floor. I let the dog out back for a few minutes while I checked my phone for any messages. I had no texts and no emails. I let the dog back inside and fed him. Then I changed into workout clothes and went for a run. Alana lived in a small neighborhood. I preferred to lap it multiple times versus running on the main road outside of her community. There were far too many cars on it, and I've seen way too many people texting while driving. It wouldn't take much for one of them to lose focus and hit me while I ran down the side of the road.

I was about halfway through my run when Alana pulled up beside me in her car. She rolled down the window.

"Get in," she said.

"What's wrong?" I asked.

"There's been a death at the Chambers Hotel. It's Joe."

I climbed into Alana's car, and we made the drive to the hotel in record time. This was one of the advantages of driving in a detective's car with flashing lights. We saw a few other police cars and one ambulance when we pulled into the hotel parking lot.

"You better stay in the lobby until I figure out what's going on," Alana said.

I followed Alana into the lobby. She spoke to one of the officers and then headed to the elevator. I looked and saw Mill Chambers standing beside another officer. I was tempted to go talk to him but resisted the urge. I walked around and did my best to eavesdrop on various conversations, hoping to overhear some information. However, no one seemed to know anything beyond the rumor that someone had died. Alana came back downstairs several minutes later. She walked up to me.

"It's Joe all right. It looks like he overdosed." Alana turned and saw Mill. "Let's see what he has to say."

Alana and I approached Mill Chambers. He looked worried, maybe even frightened.

"I'm sorry about your brother," Alana said.

Mill nodded but didn't say anything.

"The officer upstairs said you found him. Is that correct?" Alana asked.

Mill nodded a second time.

"What happened?" she asked.

"Joe sometimes spends the night here when he's had too much to drink. I get here early, so I overlap the night and day managers. The night manager told me Joe had checked himself into one of the rooms. It pissed me off because we're near capacity."

"So you went to the room to get him out?" Alana asked.

"I knocked on the door several times, but he wouldn't answer. I have a master key, so I let myself in. That's when I saw him on the bed."

"Was he still breathing when you found him?"

"I don't think so. I felt for a pulse but couldn't find one. Then I called 911."

"Did you try CPR?" she asked.

"Yes, but I'm not sure I was even doing it right. I took the class a long time ago."

"Did you come back to the lobby after that?"

"Yes. I ran right back to look for the police," Mill said.

"Another officer spoke with a front desk attendant. He said you and Joe got in a pretty nasty argument yesterday," Alana said.

"I didn't kill Joe, if that's what you're implying," Mill said.

"What caused the fight?" Alana asked.

"Joe showed up late for work, as usual. He told me I was fired since he was the new owner of the hotel. Then he started laughing at me. I told him he had no right to fire me. The operating agreement still keeps me in charge of all hotel decisions, despite what his fake will might say. He told me I needed to leave, and we started arguing."

"Did it get physical?" Alana asked.

"No, I was embarrassed by the way I behaved at my mother's wake, so I just walked away from him."

"Joe worked as the bar manager and bartender, right?" Alana asked.

"Yes."

"Was it common for him to get drunk during work?"

"Sometimes he would do shots with some of the hotel guests. I told him not to, but he knew I couldn't fire him."

"Is that because your mother wouldn't allow it?" Alana asked.

"Yeah. I actually tried to fire him once. That lasted all of a day."

"I see there are security cameras in the lobby and the hallways. I'd like to review the footage from yesterday and last night."

Mill led Alana and me to the offices behind the front desk. He tried to give Alana a quick lesson on how to go through the footage, but she already knew how to do it. Mill left us alone. It took a few minutes of rewinding the footage to find the argument between Mill and Joe in the lobby. There was no sound from the cameras, but the argument was obvious based on their facial expressions and body language. It looked like a physical fight might break out several times, but it never did. The video seemed to support Mill's version of the argument.

Alana then switched to the camera showing the hallway leading to Joe's room. We first spotted Mill approaching the door. He didn't knock on it as he described. He was slamming his fist against the door. He was yelling something, and I guessed it was "open up," but I'm not the greatest at lip reading. We then watched as Mill reached into his front pocket and removed a keycard that he used to open the door. He was in the room for several minutes before he left. Mill had said he tried CPR on Joe. I wasn't sure if he did it for those several minutes. Of course, he could have been giving Joe the overdose while Joe was passed out from too much drinking. There was also the comment Mill made about running out of the room. The video proved that to be inaccurate. He walked out of the room, and it wasn't even a hurried walk. Unfortunately, it was impossible to see the look on Mill's face from the camera angle.

Alana rewound the footage again. A few hours of footage went by and no one else appeared in the hallway. Then we saw a woman with blond hair leave Joe's room. She wore tight jeans and a tank top. Alana rewound again until the woman appeared walking down the hall, approaching Joe's door. Based on the timestamp of the footage, the woman had been in the room for a couple of hours. Alana called Mill back into the office.

"Do you recognize this woman?" Alana asked.

Mill studied the footage.

"No, I've never seen her before."

"Is the person who worked the front desk last night still here?" Alana asked.

"Yes, the police told her not to leave."

"Please send her back here."

A young woman walked into our room a few minutes later. She looked college-aged.

"Did you work last night?"

"Yes."

"Do you remember this woman coming into the hotel?"

Alana showed her a still image of the security footage.

"Yes."

"Have you seen her before?"

"She comes in from time to time. She's a friend of Joe."

"Would she ever ask you what room he was in?"

"No. She always knew. I guess Joe told her."

"How did you know she was here to see him?" Alana asked.

"I stopped her the first time she came in. I didn't recognize her."

"Do you usually recognize everyone at the hotel?" Alana asked.

"No, I thought Mill might not want her here, based on the way she was dressed that night."

"You thought she might have been a prostitute?"

The front desk attendant nodded. "She got really angry with me for stopping her. Joe yelled at me the next night. He said I had no reason to question her."

"Did you ever see her again?" Alana asked.

"Maybe once or twice in the bar. She'd have some drinks and talk to Joe while he worked."

"Do you know her name?" Alana asked.

"No, I never asked."

Alana thanked her for her time and told her she could go. Alana called Mill back into the office.

"Are there other bartenders or waiters who worked with Joe who might know this woman?" Alana asked.

"We only have one bartender on duty at a time, but I can give you the names and numbers of the two waitresses."

"Were they both working last night?"

"I think so, but I'll confirm that. Let me go check the schedule."

Mill left the room. I turned to Alana.

"When the woman left Joe's room, she probably exited through the lobby. Maybe there's a better view of her face on that camera," I said.

Alana switched to the lobby camera and reviewed the footage. We found the brief clip of the blond woman exiting the elevator and walking toward the door. There was a slightly better shot of her face, but the image was still somewhat fuzzy. It was impossible to make out a facial expression.

"Not much better," Alana said.

Alana and I stood and walked out of the offices and back to the front desk. We immediately saw Bethany and Barry in the lobby. Alana walked over to them while I stayed behind the desk. I turned to the front desk attendant.

"Can you do me a favor and burn two copies of last night's security footage to a disc?"

"Sure thing," she said.

She immediately left the desk and went into the back office. I think she was anxious to get out of the lobby. I went from behind the desk and got closer to Alana, who was now speaking to Bethany and Barry. I didn't hear what Alana asked them, but I did hear Bethany ask, "Are you implying that Mill had anything to do with this?"

"No one is implying anything here. I just wanted to know if either of you witnessed the argument between Mill and Joe yesterday."

"Joe was out of control. Everyone knew it," Bethany said.

"Mill says Joe would often spend the night here because he was drunk. Have you ever witnessed that?" Alana asked.

"What do you want from us? My brother just died!" Bethany said and burst into tears.

Barry did his best to comfort her, but there really wasn't anything he could do or say.

First Charlotte was murdered, and then Joe died of what might or might not have been an accidental drug overdose. I walked behind the front desk and into the back offices. I found the attendant copying the security files to a couple of DVDs.

"When did you find out about Joe?" I asked.

"Mill told me. He came downstairs as soon as the ambulance arrived."

"How did Mill seem?" I asked.

"I'm not sure."

"He didn't seem stressed out? He wasn't crying?"

"No, he kind of had this blank look on his face."

"Did he go outside to greet the paramedics?" I asked.

"No, he stayed in the lobby. He took them up to the room once they got inside."

The camera files finished downloading to the DVDs and the attendant handed them to me.

"Thanks," I said.

"What's going to happen now?" she asked.

"They'll do an autopsy to determine the cause of death."

"Do you think that woman had something to do with it?"

"I don't know." I held up the two DVDs. "Thanks for this."

I headed toward the lobby again, but I slipped one of the DVDs into my back pocket before I reached Alana.

"Here's a copy of the security footage. I asked the front desk lady to burn you a copy."

I handed her the DVD.

"Thanks."

"Did Mill give you the names of the two waitresses on duty last night?" I asked.

"Yeah, I'll need to check them out later today. Right now I need to get back to the office. I'll have to catch up with you later." Alana then realized my car was still at her house. "Damn, I forgot we rode in together."

"Don't worry about it," I said. "Just give me a ride to your office, and I'll either call a cab or get Foxx to pick me up."

"You sure?" she asked.

"Yeah, it's no problem. You've got enough on your plate."

I ended up taking a cab from the police station to Alana's house. I had a spare key. Yes, we'd reached that point in our relationship, so I let myself in and got the dog. I took Maui back to Foxx's house. I noticed the white sedan was gone and so was Foxx's car. I was kind of glad I was alone. It would slightly delay the inevitable Foxx-Hani conversation I was sure was coming. I walked Maui around a couple of blocks so he could do his thing. I then went into the house and loaded the DVD into my laptop. I copied the footage to my hard drive so it would play smoother. I found the clip of the blond woman in the hotel lobby. I went through it frame by frame until I found the best shot. I printed the still image. Fortunately, Foxx had a fairly nice laser printer, and the image wasn't half bad.

I said goodbye to the dog. I know; that's kind of weird, isn't it? But I'm guessing I'm not the only one who does that. I got into my convertible and drove to Candi's apartment. I wasn't sure if she'd be home, and if she was, I hoped she wouldn't be entertaining a customer. Fortunately, I caught her alone.

I knocked on her door. Based on her expression, she seemed surprised to see me, maybe even a little happy. I knew for certain, though, based on that happy expression, she hadn't heard of Joe's death yet. I sat back down on the same sofa. She sat beside me again, but not nearly as close as the last time.

"I was wondering, Candi, if you know who this person is?"

I handed Candi the photo I had printed out. She studied it for a second, and then I could see in her eyes she realized who it was.

"Why do you want to know?" she asked.

"Forgive me. I don't know how else to say this, so I'm just going to say it. Joe died sometime this morning."

"Oh, God. Oh, God." There was a long pause and then another, "Oh, God. How did it happen?"

"They think it might have been a drug overdose."

"Was she with him?" Candi asked.

"At some point. Do you recognize her?" I asked.

"It's Joe's old girlfriend, Donna. Where did it happen?"

"At the Chambers Hotel. This shot is from the security camera in the lobby. Joe was found dead in a hotel room."

I wasn't sure if that was considered sensitive information. It probably was, but I wanted a dramatic buildup to the plan I had worked out on the long drive here.

"I spoke with several employees of the hotel who worked with Joe. They said he would often get drunk and check himself into one of the empty rooms. Apparently, this Donna woman was a frequent visitor of his."

"That son of a bitch," she said.

I let Candi fume for a few seconds, and then I said, "I know Joe did drugs. Do you know if Donna did too?"

"She might have. I don't know."

"What do you know about her?" I asked.

"Not much. Joe didn't talk about her a lot. She's a waitress at a restaurant down the street from the hotel. Joe said he met her when she came into the bar after work. That's the only reason I know what she looks like. She came to the bar once when I was hanging out with Joe."

"It seems pretty clear that Joe was cheating on you. You must realize he never intended to share any of the inheritance with you."

I expected some kind of response from Candi, maybe not verbal but definitely a physical sign that would show she knew exactly what I was talking about. Of course, I wouldn't have gotten one if I had been wrong about the whole thing, but I would have bet all my dollars that I wasn't. So, did I get a reaction? Absolutely. Candi looked like she would have cut me in half had she only had a machete within reach.

"I had a handwriting expert compare Charlotte Chambers' signature to the one on the new will Joe produced. It's a very good likeness, but it's still a forgery. My guess is Joe offered to give you some of the inheritance if you claimed to have witnessed her sign it. You know that's a felony, don't you?"

Candi didn't respond this time. She no longer seemed angry, or afraid for that matter. She'd gone into survival mode.

"Of course, Dick Halverson has a lot more to lose than you do. He's going to get disbarred in addition to going to prison," I said.

"What do you want?" Candi asked.

"Information. The new will is going away, especially now that Joe is dead. Maybe I can convince Mara Winters to forget she even saw the new will, and maybe I can ask Detective Hu to drop the case against you and Halverson."

"What kind of information?" she asked.

"A few things. Am I right about the will?"

Candi nodded. "Joe promised me money for signing it. Her signature was already on it when he gave it to me. I didn't know if she signed it or not."

"But you signed it anyway."

"He gave me five grand to do it."

"Did Joe tell you if he faked his mother's signature, or did he get someone else to do it?" I asked.

"He didn't say anything about that. I didn't even know if it was a fake."

"And Dick Halverson? You were the one who put Joe in touch with him?"

"Joe gave him five grand to write the new will and sign it, too. You're wrong about Dick getting disbarred."

"Why is that?" I asked.

"Because he's already been disbarred. The guy's broke. That's why he agreed to do the deal with Joe."

"Do you know anything about Charlotte's death? Did Joe have anything to do with it?"

"No, Joe loved his mom. He said he would never have hurt her."

"Did he have an idea of who might want to harm her?" I asked.

"He said he thought his brother did it. He said the guy was the greediest person he knew and that he'd do anything to get his hands on the money."

I stood.

"Thanks, Candi, and I'm sorry about Joe. I know you cared for him."

Actually, I wasn't sure she cared for him at all, but it seemed like a nice thing to say.

"Are you really going to keep my name out of this?" she asked.

"I think I can."

I left the apartment, and as before, Candi stayed on the sofa and didn't walk me to the door. I drove past the Chambers Hotel to see if I could figure out what restaurant Donna might work at. There was only one place near the hotel. It was a mom-and-pop pizza place called Momma's.

I pulled into the parking lot, but I called Mara before I entered the restaurant. I told her about my conversation with Candi and her admission that she didn't actually witness Charlotte sign the document. I left out my little fib about the handwriting expert. I did mention that Dick Halverson had supposedly been barred from practicing law and was paid handsomely to pretend to witness Charlotte's signature. I didn't know if it was illegal for Halverson to create the will for Joe given he was technically no longer an attorney. Mara didn't mention anything about that when I told her. She just thanked me for the information, and I ended the call.

Mara had two options, at least that's the way I saw it. Option one was to pretend she never saw the fake new will. Joe was now gone, and I doubted there would be anyone else who would fight for that phony document. Option two was to move forward with legally proving the new will was based on a fake signature. I knew she couldn't base any legal decision on what I had just told her. It was all hearsay.

There was also another new question that Joe's death brought up. What happened to Joe's share of the property? Even if there was no new will, fake or otherwise, he was still entitled to a third of the

Chambers fortune. Did Joe have a will of his own? What happened to his third now that he was gone? Did it immediately get split between Mill and Bethany? Was that an additional motive for a potential murder?

I didn't know if Mill or Bethany had gotten a good look at the new will. I saw Mill look at it briefly during the wake before he tore the photocopy to pieces. Maybe he or his sister went to see Mara the next day and got a better look at the original. Mara thought the signature could pass for Charlotte's. That certainly could have also meant it fooled Mill and Jen, too. Perhaps they thought their mother had really written them out. How might they have reacted if that had been the truth? Was it strong enough to murder their brother?

Charlotte had thought one of them was responsible for the threats on her life. If they were cruel and greedy enough to kill a parent, they probably wouldn't think twice about murdering a sibling. Of course, Joe's death might simply have been an accidental overdose and the close proximity in time to his mother's death a pure coincidence. Charlotte's murderer could also very well be someone outside the family, for example, Trevor Edelman.

I pushed all these questions temporarily aside and walked into Momma's. The restaurant only had about ten tables. I saw one couple dining, but it was the middle of the afternoon, too late for the lunch crowd and too early for dinner. I walked up to a small bar near the front of the restaurant.

"May I help you?" the bartender asked.

"Yes, I'd like to order a medium pizza to go, all the fixings, please."

"You got it. Would you like a drink while you wait?"

"Sure, a Coors Lite would be great."

The bartender rang up my order and then handed me the Coors Lite.

"Would you like a glass with that?" he asked.

"No, thanks. Bottle is great."

I took a swig of the beer.

"Say, is Donna working tonight?" I asked.

"How do you know Donna?"

"I met her last night at the Chambers Hotel bar. She said she was a friend of the bartender there."

"Joe?"

"I think that was his name," I said.

"Yeah, I know Joe too. Good guy. Yeah, Donna is working tonight. Should I tell her you said hi?"

"Sure. Tell her Dick says hi."

I wasn't sure why I gave my fake name as Dick, but I'd just been talking about Dick Halverson right before I came into the restaurant. I know I told Candi I'd do my best to keep her name out of everything, but I really needed a way to nail Halverson. The guy was a fraud. He took five grand to cheat Mill and Bethany out of their legacy.

The bartender handed me the pizza about twenty minutes later. It smelled good. I paid him and left a decent tip for the beer. I walked outside and put the pizza on the passenger seat. I called Alana before I started the car.

"I was just about to call you," she said. "I spoke to the two waitresses who work with Joe at the Chambers Hotel. One of them said she thinks the girl works at an Italian restaurant."

"It's called Momma's, and the woman's name is Donna. She has a shift there tonight, but I don't know exactly what time she starts."

"Should I ask how you got this information?"

"I can fill you in later, if you want. Any word on Joe's autopsy?"

"It's scheduled for tomorrow afternoon, but we already know it was heroin. The question is, did he stick the needle in his arm or did someone do it for him," Alana said.

"If the girl supplied him the drugs or if she did them with him, can that potentially go down as murder?" I asked.

"Not sure. That's a question for the D. A."

"By the way, are you hungry? I just bought a supreme pizza."

"Maybe later. I'll need to meet up with this Donna first."

"You don't want me there?" I asked.

"No, there's something else I need to talk to you about, but I'd rather do it in person. I can swing by your place tonight, if that's okay."

"What's going on?" I asked.

"Just do me this favor and let me meet with Donna on my own."

I could tell by the tone in her voice this was an argument not worth having.

13

GAME CHANGER

I DROVE HOME, AND FOXX AND I ATE MOST OF THE PIZZA AND HAD A few beers while we watched an old movie on television called *Big Trouble in Little China*. In some ways, it was a ridiculous film, a bizarre combination of action, comedy, and fantasy, but we loved it. I'd lost count a long time ago of how many times we'd watched it together, but the film never got old for us, and we still predictably laughed at all the same places.

I managed to put aside a couple of pizza slices for Alana. The pizza was decent. It wasn't even close to being the best I had ever had, but I figured it was more than adequate for the tourist zone, which was probably the reason they were still in business. After the pizza and the movie, we grabbed some more beers and went out to the pool.

"I'm sorry I kept the Hani thing from you," Foxx said.

"No big deal."

"You mean that?" he asked.

"Yeah. You said it was nothing serious, right? It's not like you need my permission anyway."

"Hani seems to think Alana would be upset. I'm not sure if I should take that as an insult or not. Maybe Hani's embarrassed by me."

"I don't think that's it."

"Then what is it?" Foxx asked.

"You've sort of developed a reputation as a womanizer. She probably thinks Alana would be concerned by that."

"No, I haven't."

"Come on, Foxx. You're with a different girl every other week."

"That's what everyone thinks? That I'm just going to cast Hani aside once I'm bored with her?"

"Who's everyone? I thought I was the only person who knew. And no, I don't think you're going to cast her aside. I think she's going to cast you aside."

"Dump me?" Foxx asked.

"Watch your back. That's all I'm saying. You have a lot of money now. Don't be surprised if she's coming for it."

"You think I'm that naïve? You think I can't take care of myself?"

"Is this heading into an argument?" I asked.

"I don't know," Foxx said.

"Well, I don't want it to. Just know this. I'm not ever going to judge you. If you want to be with Hani, that's cool. And if you don't want me to tell Alana, I won't."

The doorbell rang at that moment, and I hoped to God that we weren't loud enough for Alana to hear us, at least I assumed it was Alana who was at the front door. Maui the dog barked and ran toward the front of the house.

"I think that's Alana," I said.

"Don't say a word about this."

"I told you I wouldn't."

It wasn't Alana, though. It was Hani. She looked fantastic, as usual.

"Hey there," Hani said.

She walked inside and bent over to pat Maui on the head. Hani looked up at me.

"Is Foxx here?"

"Yeah, he's out the back by the pool."

Hani walked toward the back of the house.

"Can I get you a beer?" I asked.

"That would be great," she said.

I walked into the kitchen and grabbed three beers. Maui the dog followed me back outside. I handed Foxx and Hani their beers.

"Alana's coming over later," I told Hani.

"Cool. I haven't seen her in a few days," Hani said.

I was a little confused by Hani. I wasn't sure if she intended to leave before Alana's arrival. If she didn't, I wasn't sure what her excuse would be for her presence. But it was their little secret, and I wasn't overly worried about it getting out. I didn't think Alana would necessarily endorse the relationship, but I also didn't think she'd be upset by it.

We all sat by the pool and watched the sunset. None of us said much. It was just a relaxing time to kick back and enjoy the beauty of Maui - the island, not the dog.

"You guys have such an amazing view here," Hani said.

"What are you up to these days?" I asked Hani.

"Still trying to figure out what I want to do."

"Understandable. Foxx and I are in the same boat."

"Not you. I heard you were basically working as an investigator for Mara," she said.

"Nothing official. I just did one case for her."

Hani laughed. "Foxx told me about that one. I can't believe that doctor would do that out in the open."

"It was a little surprising," I admitted.

"You've handled two cases, though," Foxx pointed out.

"Something tells me the Chambers case was just taken away from me," I said.

"Why's that?" Hani asked.

"I'm not sure, but I think Alana is going to let me know later tonight."

I hung out with Foxx and Hani for a few more minutes. Then I went inside to watch television. Alana arrived about thirty minutes later. She saw Hani outside with Foxx as she sat down beside me on the sofa.

"What's Hani doing here?" she asked.

"She just stopped by to say hello."

Alana shot me this look that managed to say "Don't give me that B.S. What are you holding back from me?" Yes, women have a way of communicating multiple points with one look.

"Were you able to meet up with Donna?" I asked.

"I went by the restaurant, but she called in sick tonight."

"She must have heard about Joe."

"That was my guess, too. I got her home address from the manager, and I went to see her."

"What's she like?" I asked.

"Young girl, maybe mid-twenties. She said she never dated Joe Chambers. She said they only hooked up a few times after work. She sometimes got drinks at the hotel bar. That's where she met him."

"What about the drugs?"

"I asked her that, and she said the most she ever did was smoke pot with Joe. She said he offered her the hard stuff, but she always said no."

"Did she see him doing heroin last night?" I asked.

"Not according to her. They drank a little and then had sex. She left around three in the morning, which I was able to confirm from the security camera footage."

"Is there any way to estimate a time of death for Joe?"

"The M. E. said Joe had been dead around an hour or two before Mill found him."

"When did Mill discover the body exactly?" I asked.

"He called 911 at seven fourteen. I verified that with the phone records. The security camera footage shows him going into the room at five after seven."

"He sat there and looked at Joe's dead body for nine minutes?"

"Apparently," Alana said.

"And the M. E. said Joe died a couple of hours before that?" I asked.

"Yes, he estimates the time of death was between five and seven in the morning."

"How does he estimate that? Is it body temperature?"

"That's one of the indicators. There are other indicators, like rigor mortis."

"That must clear Mill and Donna," I said.

"Joe's fingerprints were the only ones on the syringe. There was also a small plastic bag of drugs on the nightstand. His prints were the only ones on that, too."

"So even if Donna brought Joe the drugs, she was careful enough to wipe her prints off."

"I doubt she did that. I got a good look at her arms while I was talking to her. I didn't see any indication of drug use, at least nothing that would leave needle marks. Plus, I don't think she had anything to gain by Joe's death. She seemed pretty shaken up by it all. On the other hand, she could just be a good actor."

"I still don't understand why Mill waited so long to call an ambulance," I said.

"Maybe he wanted to make sure Joe was really dead."

"Who knows? Maybe he even considered not calling at all, but he thought it through and realized his image would be all over the security footage. It wasn't like he could selectively erase anything without making himself look guilty."

I realized we were doing some major guess work here. The truth was Mill might just have been in serious shock. The guy had just walked in on his dead brother, lying on a bed with a needle sticking out of his arm. He might have had major issues with Joe, maybe he even hated him, but that didn't mean he wanted him dead.

"Do you know how the department's going to rule this?" I asked.

"Probably an accidental death. That's not official, though."

"What was it you wanted to talk to me about earlier?"

"I got a call from Mara Winters right before you called me, and she told me about your meeting with Candi. Mill and Bethany have lawyered up. Mara informed me that I'm not to interview any members of the Chambers family without her present."

"What does that have to do with me being there for your conversation with Donna?" I asked.

"Mara's not exactly a friend of the department," Alana said. "Anyway, after her call, the captain had a change of heart regarding your involvement. He wants you out of this."

I nodded. It wasn't like this was a major surprise. I didn't see it coming, exactly, but it wasn't unpredictable either.

"Of course, as long as you aren't breaking any laws, the department can't tell you what you can and can't do with your time," she said.

I knew what Alana was really saying. She realized I was probably going to continue my own investigation. She knew she couldn't stop me, but she was requesting that I not make her life difficult by asking her to bail me out of trouble.

"I get it," I said.

Alana turned from me and looked outside. Hani and Foxx were laughing.

"They're having sex, aren't they?" she asked.

I said nothing. Alana turned back to me.

"How long have you known about this?" she asked.

"Known about what?"

"What do you think I'm talking about? Did you make some kind of promise to Foxx or Hani not to speak to me about it?"

"I haven't technically seen the sex, so I can't answer your question with any reliability."

"You sound like Mara Winters. Does Foxx know about Hani's issues with telling the truth?" Alana asked.

"I'm sure he does."

"And does Hani know about Foxx's issues with not being able to commit to someone?"

"I'm sure she does."

"What happens to us when my sister and your best friend end up hating each other after the messy breakup?" she asked.

"Let's just hope there isn't one."

"You really think this is going to last?"

"Not a chance. But maybe they'll both be adult enough to acknowledge what it is and just let it end on a peaceful note," I said.

"And what is this relationship exactly?"

"Two people who have both lost someone and are giving each other comfort."

"By comfort, you mean sex?"

"Exactly."

"Okay, we'll just see how it goes."

"Are you going to let on that you know?" I asked.

"What would be the point? I'm not sure why they didn't want me to know, but I think it will be fun watching them come up with excuses for why they keep bumping into each other."

"Did you tell Hani you were coming here tonight?" I asked.

"She called me a few hours ago. I might have mentioned it."

"Then there you go. This is her way of telling you without having to actually tell you."

Alana stood and walked outside. I followed her, but I had no idea what she was about to do.

"You guys want to double date tomorrow? We could do burgers at Harry's or something," Alana said.

"You told her, didn't you?" Foxx asked.

I shook my head.

"He didn't say anything. My guess is you started this the night of the party. Is that right?" Alana asked.

Neither Foxx nor Hani said a word.

"You guys were really into each other that night. It was obvious, and you were drinking. I'd say one thing led to another..." Alana continued.

Foxx laughed. "Poe said you were one smart lady."

Alana turned to me and smiled. "You said that?"

"Yep."

I hoped that my comment had just scored me major brownie points. Alana turned back to Foxx and Hani.

"There's no reason to keep secrets between us," she said.

Foxx held up his beer as if in a toast. Alana turned back to me.

"Did you and Foxx eat all that pizza, or did you save me a slice?"

"I saved you *two* slices," I said.

"Poe wanted to eat them, but I told him not to," Foxx said.

"Thank you, Foxx, and my stomach thanks you, too, because I'm starving."

14

THE FUNERAL – PART 2

I DIDN'T HAVE MUCH PERSONAL INVOLVEMENT IN THE CHAMBERS' CASE over the next few days. I spent most of my time either walking the dog, going on long runs, or photographing the island. I'd shot just about every place on the island more than once, but Maui is so beautiful and always worth multiple photographs. I think I could spend the rest of my life here and never get tired of it.

Alana was good enough to keep me apprised of the case. Much of her attention seemed to be on nailing Candi and Dick Halverson for their role in Joe's false will.

Alana said they scared the hell out of Candi for her involvement. Apparently, it's a felony to falsely claim to witness a signature. Candi had already been arrested a couple of times before, so she was looking at serious jail time. She was offered immunity, though, if she was willing to testify against Dick Halverson for his part in lying about witnessing Charlotte's signature. I think the D. A. viewed Candi as small potatoes. It was much better publicity for the department to be seen taking down a disbarred attorney who was still practicing law creating fake wills and fraudulently certifying witnessed signatures for cash under the table.

I expected to get an angry phone call from Candi. After all, I had implied to her that the police would probably just drop the matter. Yeah, I was seriously wrong about that one. I didn't intentionally mislead her. We'll just have to chalk that one up to a case of me being really naïve. At least Candi's record was cleared, and she wasn't going to serve jail time. By record, I mean the matter of the fake will and not her previous arrests for prostitution.

I didn't touch base with Mara Winters regarding the will. I knew she'd refuse to discuss client issues with me, and I certainly understood and respected that position. I imagine, though, that the will Joe produced was now considered null and void, and that they'd go back to the last will Charlotte was known to have actually signed. That will gave the Chambers fortune to Mill, Bethany, and Joe, all in equal parts.

Now that Joe was gone, I didn't know how Joe's share would be distributed. Maybe Joe had a will of his own, and he could have potentially left his share to someone else. As far as I knew, he'd never been married and had no children. I wasn't sure if there was even someone outside the immediate family whom he would want to leave anything to. Let's face it, he didn't like anyone in his immediate family, either. He struck me as being a serious mess, so I couldn't see him having the foresight to create a will of his own.

There was little to no progress made on the investigation into Charlotte's death. The case turned cold, and Alana admitted to me that she had no idea where or how to generate new leads. It was a serious embarrassment to her because the media was constantly demanding updates. Charlotte had been a well-known member of the Maui community. Her murder had to be solved.

Joe's funeral was held about a week after his accidental overdose, and that's exactly how the D. A. ruled it, probably to the great relief of Mill and Donna.

Joe was buried in a plot beside his parents. I went to the funeral by myself. I must be honest with you and freely admit that I didn't want to go. I felt no connection to Joe at all, but I went out of a sense of obligation. I'm not sure why I felt that sense of obligation. I just did. So I broke out the dark suit for a second time.

I was one of just a few people at the funeral. Neither Mill nor Bethany attended, which I found appalling, despite their feelings toward their brother and his role in trying to defraud them. Maybe I'm too forgiving, or maybe it's unfair of me to have expected them to come. But it wasn't like he could do anything to steal from them now. What would it have hurt to pay their respects? Surely there had to have been some moments when they all loved and cared for each other.

Candi and Donna were also no-shows. Maybe they were worried they'd run into each other. Perhaps Donna didn't want to be associated with Joe in any way anymore. I couldn't blame her, and I guessed Candi felt too betrayed by Joe to attend. On the other hand, Candi and Joe had had an open relationship. It wasn't like Candi was faithful either. The woman worked as a prostitute. She still worked as one as far as I knew.

The minister who presided over Joe's funeral was the same guy who had handled Charlotte's. He used almost the same exact speech, confirming my earlier suspicion that he used a Mad Libs template to officiate these things. "We lay INSERT NAME to rest. May God bless and watch over INSERT NAME's soul."

I scanned the few attendees' faces during the service. There was only one person I recognized - Trevor Edelman. I'm pretty sure he saw me, too. Hell, he couldn't have missed me. Neither of us said anything or even acknowledged the other person's presence, but I was curious as to why he was even there. It was my understanding that he hated the Chambers family. He didn't come to Charlotte's funeral, at least I don't remember seeing him there, so why had he come to Joe's? I made a mental note to explore that later. I didn't think speaking to him about it there was either the right place or time. There was no wake afterward, either.

I drove to Harry's after the funeral and grabbed a beer by myself. I asked the bartender for a pen, and I wrote down some notes regarding everything I had learned about the case. I also did this on my two previous murder investigations. It was a way to potentially discover new thoughts and theories.

Charlotte first went to Mara after receiving two letters that threatened her life. She also thought someone may have tried to kill her by slipping something into her wine. She thought that may have caused her to fall asleep while in the tub. Unfortunately, Charlotte poured the rest of the bottle down the drain. Other wine bottles in Charlotte's pantry were tested, and none of them had contained anything out of the ordinary. Charlotte indicated three potential suspects, her children Mill, Bethany, and Joe. My initial reaction to Charlotte's story was that she was an elderly woman who had too much wine to drink and simply fell asleep in a hot bath. However, the threatening note at the party changed all that. The killer, apparently no longer content with the subtle way to murder Charlotte, struck her in the back of the head and then threw her into the swimming pool.

Mill and Jen provided alibis for each other. They claimed they were at home watching television. Bethany and her husband Barry claimed the same thing. The alibis meant nothing to me. It was natural and completely expected for spouses to cover for each other. Maybe one of the spouses was even in on it, too. Joe Chambers claimed he was home alone. He had no alibi. Of course, that didn't mean he did it.

Jen pointed out that Trevor Edelman might have murdered Charlotte. Trevor is the son of Millard Senior's former partner. The partners had a major falling out for unknown reasons. Trevor owned a boat-building company that looked like it wasn't doing so well. I couldn't see him rolling in money. Trevor confronted Mill because he felt the Chambers family ripped off his family and owed them a portion of the potential sale of the hotel. Trevor claimed he was at work alone the night of the murder.

Joe unveiled a new will that left him the entire estate. He even felt the need to show his brother a copy of the will at their mother's wake. It was an unbelievably cold, callous, and insensitive thing to do. Did that make him a killer or just a world-class jerk?

Joe's two witnesses for his mother signing the will were his prostitute girlfriend and a disgraced ex-lawyer. I know I keep referring to her as a prostitute. Does that make me judgmental? Probably. But this wasn't a case of Julia Roberts with a heart of gold. If you end up as a prostitute in real life, chances are you've made some seriously bad choices in life. One could, at least, fairly judge you for the quality of your decision-making ability. I think it's more than safe to say that if you've turned to prostitution, you're capable of breaking the law in other ways. After all, Candi played a pivotal role in trying to deprive Mill and Bethany of their rightful inheritance.

Joe Chambers accidentally killed himself by overdosing on heroin in one of the Chambers Hotel rooms. His brother discovered the body but took almost ten full minutes to call 911. Why? Was he in a state of shock or was he trying to determine if Joe was really dead before he called for help?

The medical examiner's estimate on Joe's time of death seemed to clear Mill and Donna. A new thought popped into my head as I made these notes on the cocktail napkin. Perhaps Joe's death was neither murder nor accidental. Maybe it was Joe committing suicide because he felt guilty over his mother's murder. I quickly dismissed that random thought, when I remembered Joe's part in crafting the false will. Anyone who was capable of doing that couldn't have too much of a conscience.

Mill and Bethany lawyered up after the death of their brother. I couldn't blame them. Two Chambers deaths in just a couple of weeks, and there were millions of dollars at stake. They knew the police were looking hard at them. Hiring Mara Winters was the sensible thing to do.

So where was I now that I had written down these notes? The answer, nowhere. No new ideas popped forth that were worth serious consideration. I knew I could re-interview Charlotte's children, but I'd get in serious trouble with Mara, not to mention Alana. However, no one warned me against interviewing any of the grandchildren. I thought Mill's twin boys might have already flown back to San Francisco, but Bethany's daughter, Olivia, lived on the island. She'd started a wedding planning company. Maybe she could provide some insight into all of this.

I ordered another beer and called Alana.

"Hey, anything interesting going on?" I asked.

"Nothing. What about you?"

"Same. Nothing."

"Where are you? I hear noise in the background," Alana said.

"Harry's. I'm having a couple of beers. Want to get together later tonight?" I asked.

"Sure. I'll give you a call when I get off work."

Alana ended the call, and I took another sip of beer. It was a fairly pointless phone call. I guess I could have sent her a text instead, but sometimes you just want to hear your lover's voice.

15

OLIVIA WILLIAMS

OLIVIA'S WEDDING PLANNING COMPANY WAS LOCATED IN LAHAINA. IT was one of four or five businesses that occupied a small two-story building a few blocks back from Front Street. I entered the building and saw Olivia sitting behind a large desk, talking on the phone. The walls of her office were covered with colorful photographs of various weddings. I looked at several of them while I waited for her to finish her call. Some of them were taken at various resorts in the area. Others were shot on the beach. Almost all of them looked like they were taken around sunrise or sunset. I heard her end her call and turned to her.

"Hello, there. Can I help you?" she asked.

"Yes, my name's Poe. I'm -"

"I saw you at my grandmother's funeral," she interrupted.

"That's right. My condolences for the loss of your grandmother and your uncle. It's so sad."

"Yes, it is, and thank you for attending the funeral."

"It was no effort."

"Well, what brings you here? Did you come by just to offer your condolences or are you planning a wedding?"

"Not exactly. Well, maybe, if all goes according to plan."

"I'm not sure I understand," she said.

I didn't understand myself, either, but I'd gotten into the bad habit of making up these little stories on the fly to justify my presence wherever it was I found myself. One of these days my imagination was going to fail me and I'd end up falling flat on my face.

"Your grandmother told me about your business. She was quite proud of you, by the way. I was wondering if you had any relationships with a jeweler. I'm shopping for a ring but don't want to find myself in a store that doesn't have the quality I'm looking for. I also don't want to be overcharged."

"Have you thought about purchasing online? There are quite a few excellent websites I could recommend."

"I've considered it, but I think I'd rather be able to see the ring in person before making a final decision."

"I completely understand. There's one jeweler in town I recommend. He's quite good, and his prices are reasonable. Do you know what kind of ring you're looking to buy?" she asked.

"An engagement ring," I said.

"I assumed as much, but I meant what kind of cut. Solitaire, emerald, princess cut..."

"I don't know much about any of them. Is there a style you recommend?" I asked.

"You should consider the Asscher cut. It's very beautiful. It's a cut you don't see every day. Unfortunately, you're going to pay more for it, but if she's a special lady..."

"Asscher cut," I repeated to myself.

"I'll write it down for you, along with the name of the jeweler."

She reached into her desk drawer and removed a small pad of paper. Olivia wrote down a few lines and tore the top sheet off. I walked over to her desk, and she handed me the paper.

"Thanks," I said.

"And who is the lucky lady you intend on proposing to?" she asked.

"Her name's Alana."

"I don't suppose you have a photo of her on your phone."

I pulled my phone out and showed her a shot of Alana on the beach.

"She's quite beautiful," Olivia said.

"Yes, she is."

"You seem like a clever man. A clever man would snatch her up before any competitors came knocking."

I knew she was setting me up with the false compliment, but I couldn't resist the bait.

"And why do you think I'm clever?" I asked.

"I saw you pick up the torn paper at the funeral when my uncles got into a fight. You were close to them, but you chose not to step in and stop them. You picked up the paper while everyone was distracted."

There were numerous things I could have said or asked in response to her observation, such as "Why were you looking at me when you should have been watching them?" Instead, I said nothing.

"Your fiancée-to-be is the detective on my grandmother's case?"

I nodded.

"I believe my family's attorney is supposed to be present when questioning is to be done," she said.

"Technically, that's right, but I'm not with the police."

"And you just swung by to ask me about jewelers."

"Exactly."

"Do you really plan on proposing to her?"

"Why? Do you doubt it?" I asked.

"Because I'd be really disappointed if you made the whole thing up and were just using your relationship to get me to open up about my grandmother or uncle."

"Are we putting all our cards on the table now?" I asked.

"Yes. Let's."

"I've thought about proposing for the last few weeks. I find myself searching online more and more for rings, but it's not an easy decision. It's quite nerve-wracking, actually."

"One of very few disadvantages of being a male," she said.

"I didn't lie about the ring, but clearly it's not the main reason for my visit. I did want to ask you about your grandmother."

"At last, the truth. Why didn't you just say so?" Olivia asked.

You might be thinking right about now that I must have been feeling like an idiot. The lady had clearly outsmarted me, but I actually found the conversation stimulating.

"I only knew your grandmother a few days before she passed. It certainly wasn't enough time to get to know her beyond any superficial observations."

"What were those superficial observations, if I may ask?"

"She seemed like a strong lady. She obviously had a lot of pride."

"Obviously. What else?"

"She was stubborn, and the truth is she might still be alive today if she'd listened to my advice and not fired her security team."

"Her death made you mad," Olivia suggested.

"On multiple levels. It was pointless and cruel, and I'm determined to figure out who did it."

"My parents said the police think someone in the family is responsible," Olivia said.

"Only because your grandmother first made the suggestion. She thought someone drugged her wine."

"Did they?"

"Perhaps. That part of the story is a bit farfetched, but I would be foolish to dismiss it out of hand."

"But you can't prove it," she said.

"No."

"My grandmother was a complex person, but most people are. Being a grandchild, I only knew her from a narrow perspective. It was impossible for me to see her as others outside the family did."

"Does that mean you don't know anyone who might have wanted to harm her?" I asked.

"I've heard of another man, someone named Edelman or something like that, who thinks he's entitled to my family's money."

"Is there anyone else?" I asked.

"Not that I know of," she said.

"Your grandmother never made any comments about someone

being mad at her or threatening her in any way?"

"No, but I doubt she would have. Your superficial observations, as you put it before, were quite correct. She was a strong lady, and she liked to project that strength at all times. She never would have admitted she was afraid of anyone or anything, especially to a younger member of the family. The truth is that I think you're wasting your time. You'll never bring the person responsible to justice."

"Why is that?" I asked.

"Because he's already dead," Olivia said.

"You're talking about your Uncle Joe."

"Yes, I saw him arguing with my grandmother on the night of the party."

"I don't remember seeing you there," I said.

"I was only there a short time. After the argument, I figured there was going to be serious family drama, so I left. I may have been gone before you even got there. I don't know. There were a lot of people there."

"What were they arguing about?" I asked.

"She walked in on him doing drugs at her house, of all places. He'd promised her he was clean, but everyone knew he wasn't. She told him she was going to fire him from the hotel and cut him off financially. She said she didn't know of any other way to get him clean."

"What was his response?"

"He just laughed at her. He said he knew she was bluffing, and then he said she felt way too guilty to ever cut him off."

"Do you know what he was talking about?" I asked.

"No idea. My uncle and my grandmother had a very toxic relationship. She made excuses for him and gave him the financial support he needed to survive. In return, he gave her the adulation she craved."

"It's one thing to be a junkie. It's quite another to commit matricide," I said.

"You might be right, but I still think he did it. It's not like he hasn't been violent with other family members before."

"Did he ever hurt you?" I asked.

"No, but my mother said he beat her for years until she met my father and he put a stop to it."

"Did you ever personally witness him hurt your mother?"

"No, but it happened before I was born and when I was very young. It's not something I think my mother or father would lie about."

"I don't think so either. Did you ever see him be so violent with someone that you thought he could be capable of murder?"

"No, I've been in L. A. the last fifteen years, though. I've only been back a year now, and I've spent most of that time trying to get this business off the ground. I haven't seen my family much at all."

I looked around the room again at all of the wedding photos hanging on the walls.

"Looks like you've done a good job of that," I said.

"I'm getting there. Maybe I'll be able to hire some help soon."

I turned back to her.

"If you knew these things about your uncle, why didn't you go to the police?" I asked.

"I wanted to. I went to my parents with the information, and they told me they'd look into it."

"Do you know if they did?" I asked.

"I don't know, honestly. I asked them about it again, and they said he was somewhere else the night my grandmother was killed."

"And where was that?"

"They said he was with his girlfriend, if you can call her that."

"If she wasn't his girlfriend, then what do you think she was?"

"Now you're not being honest with me again. Don't try to be too clever. We both know what that woman is."

"Sorry, but just for the record, I think Candi was his girlfriend."

"Candi, I wonder if she spells it with a *k* to be unique."

"Actually, she spells it with a *c* but it ends with an *i*."

"I assumed it had to be something like that," she said.

"Thanks for your time."

"No problem. If you do get engaged, do me a favor and come back here for the wedding planning."

"Of course," I said.

I left the store feeling like I had gotten my butt stomped by Olivia. I decided to walk to Harry's since it was only a few blocks away. The bar was only half full when I got there. I slipped onto a stool at the bar and ordered a beer.

There was a lot of the conversation with Olivia that stuck out to me. The first thing was obvious. The lady was quite smart. Second, Joe was apparently physically abusive to women. He'd beaten up his sister more than once. Did that mean he was willing to hurt, and ultimately kill, his mother? Had her death been an accident? Could they have gotten into an argument at Charlotte's house, and he pushed her? Perhaps he freaked out and fled, leaving his mother to drown in the pool. That didn't explain, however, the deep cut on her head. That had been caused by her being struck with a sharp object. It wasn't the result of her falling down and hitting her head on the pavement around the pool.

The third observation was that Bethany and Barry Williams didn't feel the need to report to the police that Joe had been in an argument with Charlotte during the party. I didn't know why they protected him like that, especially considering Bethany's past with Joe. You'd think she would be the first person to suspect her brother of violence.

The fourth observation was a rather small part of the conversation with Olivia but one I found potentially more interesting than any of the others. Joe had told his mother that she was too guilty to ever cut off his finances. What in the world did she have to feel guilty about, and how did that guilt relate to Joe? Did the cause of that guilt, whatever it was, have anything to do with Charlotte's murder?

I thought about calling Alana and reporting my conversation to her, but she'd technically warned me off the case. I didn't really have anything concrete to begin with anyway. It was just a theory, and it was more Olivia's than mine. I finished my beer quickly and decided to explore the reason of Charlotte's guilt. There was only one place I knew to look, her house.

16

THE KEY

I DROVE TO CHARLOTTE'S NEIGHBORHOOD AND PARKED A FEW BLOCKS from her house. I approached the house from the beach. Her back-yard was fairly secluded, and I hoped no one saw me walk onto her property.

I'd been training fairly regularly on picking locks. Alana had informed me that anyone could learn how on YouTube. I'm really not that computer literate, and I keep forgetting that you can pretty much learn anything on that website. I wouldn't be surprised if there was someone somewhere who had uploaded a video on how to perform brain surgery.

I had found several videos on how to pick a lock. I watched a couple, but ended up clicking off of them because they were so poorly shot. The third video looked like it was professionally done, at least I could make out what the person was actually saying. The video said a two-year-old could learn to pick a lock in under a minute. I was hoping that was an extreme exaggeration since it took me around twenty to thirty minutes to pick my first one. I'd gotten considerably better at it, though, and I was able to get inside Char-lotte's house in under three minutes.

As soon as I walked through the door, I realized there might have been an alarm system. I stopped and waited for the inevitable blare, but nothing came. I shut the door behind me and then realized I wasn't really sure how to begin. The problem was, I didn't know what exactly I was looking for.

The ultimate reason for me being there was that all three of Charlotte's grown children had seriously conflicting versions of what they thought Charlotte wanted in regards to her will. They painted pictures that could only be true if there were multiple Charlottes. That meant someone had to either be lying or just in serious denial of what his or her mother really wanted. That didn't necessarily mean Charlotte had those mixed feelings as well. Maybe Mill, Bethany, and Joe simply saw things the way they wanted to see them. Nevertheless, I was here, and I decided I might as well snoop around.

I started upstairs in Charlotte's bedroom. Yes, I know exactly what you're thinking, and I felt incredibly guilty for violating her privacy, but I rationalized by remembering that her murder might never be solved unless I could uncover something, anything really. I was desperate, and isn't there a saying about desperate people doing desperate things?

I went through her nightstand and found nothing out of the ordinary. I searched every drawer and under every article of clothing. I went through the closet, but there was nothing beyond dresses, shoes, and hats. I looked through the spare bedrooms, their closets, even the master bathroom and the bathroom down the hall. I found nothing interesting.

I went back downstairs and searched through her office. There were several file folders in a large cabinet. I looked through each folder and confirmed everything was related to hotel operations, just as I expected. I looked through her desk and found more folders, all hotel stuff and nothing more. I stood and walked over to the books on her shelf. There were no mysterious objects hidden in their pages.

I walked back to her desk and flipped through the pages on her desk calendar. She had one of those old-style ones that covered a large portion of her desk. There was nothing hidden between the pages of the months. I lifted up the calendar and found two pieces of white paper underneath. Each piece had two creases as if they'd been folded to fit inside an envelope. There was no envelope there, however.

Each page had one line of black type on the top. One line said, "You aren't innocent." The other line asked, "Who is the real monster?"

They weren't threatening by any means, at least not an overt threat of bodily harm, but they had to be from the same person or persons who sent the other letters.

Charlotte had hidden them under her calendar versus throwing them away like the others. Why did she do that? I didn't know why she hadn't told me about these or given them to Alana so she could dust them for fingerprints.

Then a thought occurred to me. Charlotte had already mentioned these letters when we spoke in Mara's office. These were very likely the two original letters, and Charlotte had lied about what they actually said to make her case sound more dire.

I looked at the two lines again.

You aren't innocent. Who is the real monster?

I didn't know what Charlotte had done or what this person thought she had done to warrant those kinds of messages. I took photos of the pages with my phone and placed the calendar back over them.

I walked into the living room, but there was really nothing to search. All I saw was a sofa and two chairs, no drawers, cabinets or trunks. The kitchen was my last stop. I searched through the pantry first. I saw the empty space on one of the shelves where we'd removed the remaining wine bottles for testing.

I then walked back into the kitchen and went through the drawers and cabinets. I found a couple of wine bottle openers, forks, knives, spoons, plates, bowls and pots and pans.

The last drawer I came to could best be described as a junk drawer. I think most of us have one of these in the kitchen. It's usually filled with batteries, receipts we shouldn't throw away, paperclips, rolls of masking tape, the odd coin or two, and maybe a knife or razor blade. Charlotte's junk drawer was no different. I pulled everything out and placed it on the counter. Then I saw it, a single key tucked in the back of the drawer. It had been hidden under the mess. I pulled the key out and saw it was attached to a key ring. The key ring was attached to a small, circular piece of cardboard with the number 604 written on it. I didn't remember seeing anything in the house that could have referred to that number. I thought 604 must have identified a locker or storage unit.

I pulled out my cell phone and Googled "storage units in Maui." A few different places popped up. One of them was located just a few miles away from the house. I called the office number listed on their website.

"Yes, may I help you?" the woman asked.

"Yes, my name is Mill Chambers. My mother, Charlotte Chambers, passed away a couple of weeks ago. I just found a key in her belongings that I believe may be for her storage unit. I can't remember if she used your location or another. Can you verify whether she was a customer of yours?"

"One second, Mr. Chambers."

I could hear the woman typing on a keyboard.

"I'm sorry, but we don't have any records of your mother having a unit here."

"Thank you," I said.

I ended the call and went back to the Google results on my phone. I tried the next-closest storage unit. This one was located near the airport. It wouldn't have been a very convenient location for her to use, though. I repeated my speech and got the news that Charlotte Chambers did rent a unit there.

I slipped my phone and the key into my pocket. Then I placed all the miscellaneous items back into the junk drawer. I looked around the kitchen. Everything seemed to be in place. I closed and locked the back door behind me. No one was on the beach, and I hoped my luck would hold as I exited Charlotte's backyard and walked down the public beach.

I found the storage unit complex easily. I parked in the small lot in front of their office. Fortunately, there were no customers inside. There was only one person working behind the counter. He was a young guy, maybe barely out of high school.

"Hi, I'm Mill Chambers. I called you earlier about my mother's storage unit." I pulled the key out of my pocket. "I believe she had unit 604. Could I get the code to drive my car into the complex?"

"Sure thing. I just need to see some I.D."

I paused a moment. It wasn't like the request for the I.D. was a major surprise. I had hoped the knowledge of the unit and the key would have been enough. I removed my wallet and pulled five twenties out. I fanned them out and laid them on the counter in front of the young clerk.

"Unfortunately, I forgot my driver's license," I said.

He looked at the money on the counter. Then he looked up at me. "I think I saw your I.D. when you opened your wallet."

Smart kid. I reached back into my wallet and removed another hundred dollars. I placed the notes on the previous stack of money on the counter.

"I think you're mistaken. I left my I.D. in my other pair of pants, and I promise not to remove anything from the unit. I just want to see what my dearly departed mother kept there."

The clerk casually picked up the money and slipped the stack of twenty-dollar bills into his pocket.

"Star 555. Then the pound symbol. Then 604."

"Thanks."

"Unit 604 is in the last row."

"Thanks, again."

"No problem, Mr. Chambers. Sorry for the loss of your mother."

I left the office and went back to my car. I punched the code into the security keypad by the metal gate. The gate rose slowly, and I drove to the last row of units. I found 604 about halfway down the lane. I parked in front of the door and got out. The key worked, and I pulled the door up. It squeaked and groaned like it hadn't been opened in a long time. Of course, they always sound like that.

The unit was half full at best. It mostly contained boxes of old clothes, a couple of chairs, and a few bicycles that looked like they were kids' bikes from an older age. Maybe they had once belonged to Mill, Bethany, and Joe...and Charlotte didn't have the heart to throw them away.

I searched through all her clothes and boxes of VHS tapes of movies I remembered but hadn't seen in forever. She had boxes of old kitchenware, stuff that looked worthless and broken, and things that should have been tossed or donated a long time ago.

I grew more and more frustrated with every worthless box I opened.

I looked through a box of old newspaper clippings. There were articles on the Chambers Hotel, as well as the occasional story on one of her kids. I saw that Mill's junior high school basketball team had won the Maui championship, and Bethany had won some state-wide essay contest.

I came across a stack of several shoe boxes. I opened the first two boxes and found the expected shoes. They were hideous by the way.

I leaned against the wall of the storage unit. Whatever secrets this lady held had apparently gone to the grave with her. To make matters even more depressing, I had paid the clerk two hundred bucks to go through Charlotte's junk.

I was about to leave the unit when I looked down at the last few shoe boxes. I bent over and tore off the lids. Two of the three had shoes in them just like the other boxes. The third box, however, was filled with several letters and a couple of yellowed photographs.

The letters were handwritten. The handwriting was small and neat. One of the photographs was of two people, Charlotte and a man I didn't recognize, not immediately that is. The second photograph was of Charlotte, the same man as in the other photograph, and a new man. This new guy looked a lot like Mill, so I guessed he was the first Millard Chambers.

I looked back at the first photograph. Then I looked at the second one again. The original guy had a striking resemblance to Joe Chambers. The clothing and hairstyle was a lot older, but the facial structure was similar. The dead giveaway, though, was the eyes. The most probable conclusion was that Charlotte had an affair with this man, and Joe Chambers was the result. Maybe Mill and Bethany knew the truth. It would explain their animosity toward their younger sibling.

I remembered Candi telling me that Joe had told her his brother and sister had "hated him since his birth." Perhaps they were well aware of their mother's infidelity from the time of her pregnancy.

I pulled out my phone and took photos of the two yellowed photographs. I then put the photos back in the shoebox and removed the letters. I read them all. Their contents confirmed my theory and gave a clue to the identity of the mystery man. He signed his name with one letter – E.

E confessed his love for Charlotte in each beautifully written letter. He repeatedly asked her to leave Mill for him. He promised to take care of her, to treasure her, to take her away from the source of her pain and misery, but the letters gave no indication of what caused that pain and misery.

I read them each twice. If I didn't feel guilty for violating Charlotte's privacy before, I did now. I felt horrible, and I wasn't even sure if this was related to her murder in anyway. Yes, it explained Joe's feelings of being an outcast in the Chambers family, and maybe those lifelong feelings resulted in him killing his own mother and forging her will. On the other hand, maybe Charlotte held a special place in her heart for Joe. He was the result of her affair with this man. He loved Charlotte. There were no letters from Charlotte, though, returning the feelings. Had she regretted her affair? Was she tempted to run away with him? Why had she stayed with Millard if she ultimately loved this other man?

I put the letters back in the shoebox. I then put the lids back on all the boxes and stacked them as I had found them. I looked around the storage unit. Everything looked like it was in its place, but I wasn't sure if Mill or Bethany even knew about the unit. If they had, they probably would have taken the letters and two photos and either hidden them away in their own houses or destroyed them. I shut the door and then relocked it. I climbed into my car and turned the air conditioner on full blast. It had been really hot inside the unit, and I was drenched in sweat. Only hot air blew out. I had forgotten the AC had quit on me during the slow drive to Charlotte's funeral.

During my drive home, all I could think about was my conversations with Charlotte regarding her late husband. Her entire reason for not selling the hotel was because she had wanted to honor Millard's request not to sell the business. She threw a party to honor what would have been his ninetieth birthday. Yes, it had been my idea as a way to get all of the members of the Chambers family together, but Charlotte had still spent our time together at the event praising Millard. She told me her husband had been a genius. He had designed their impressive house on a napkin. He had designed the hotel himself. She had painted a picture of him as a Renaissance man. What had led this woman to cheat on a man like that? Had she always viewed him in that glowing light, or was her commitment to him the result of him giving her a second chance?

I got home and went immediately to my laptop. I Googled everything I could find on Trevor Edelman, hoping to learn the name of his father. Finally, I found something. His name had been Edward. Edward Edelman. Double E's. He had to be the author of those love letters. Charlotte had had an affair with her husband's partner, the man Millard ultimately had a huge falling out with and the man whom Millard forced out of the hotel and paid pennies for his shares. Everything made sense now. It had to have been the affair. Millard found out Charlotte was sleeping with Edelman. He'd even gotten her pregnant. No wonder Millard kicked him out. I would have done the same. I'd have done a hell of a lot more, actually.

I didn't know how Millard could have forgiven Charlotte. Perhaps he didn't know the baby was Edelman's. Maybe Charlotte had slept with them both and managed to convince Millard the baby was his, although that secret wouldn't have stayed a secret for very long. Joe looked nothing like Mill and Bethany. Millard Senior would have had to have been a blind man to not see that.

Again, I thought of calling Alana and telling her this family secret, but what did it really reveal other than a dark chapter in Charlotte's hisstory? I came back to the same dilemma I had thought about in the storage unit. None of this proved anything in terms of her murder.

I sat on the information regarding Joe's real father, at least who I thought was Joe's father, for a few days. I really wasn't sure what to do with it. I'd seen Alana each of those days. I knew she was frustrated with her lack of progress on the case, but I couldn't shake the feeling that this secret was nothing more than a family scandal. Yes, it was a big family scandal. However, it didn't seem possible that it could be connected to Charlotte's murder. Alana was being pulled in other directions, too. It wasn't like all other law enforcement business stopped on the island just so she could focus all of her attention on solving the riddle of Charlotte Chambers' murder.

I spent the next week not doing much of anything. I thought about driving around the island and taking more photos, but then I'd get discouraged and not do it.

I hung out with Foxx several times at Harry's. The subject of Hani never came up during our conversations. I wasn't sure if that meant they had already decided to cool things off or if things were actually getting more serious, but he didn't want to tell me. I assumed it was the latter because he never hit on any women during those long sessions at the bar. That was unlike him.

I spent the mornings swimming laps in the pool and just lounging in the sun. I knew it was terribly indulgent of me, but I was depressed over my failure to solve the case, and the sun kept me from plunging into deeper misery.

When I wasn't at the bar or swimming in the pool, I took the dog for long walks, hoping some small but significant detail that only my subconscious had registered would pop up and everything would suddenly become clear. Unfortunately, that didn't happen.

I did, however, manage to piss off one of the neighbors when he saw Maui the dog pooping in his yard. I already had the plastic bag in my hand, but the guy started banging on the narrow glass window beside his door. This, of course, startled my dog, who immediately got uptight and couldn't finish his business in a timely fashion. That delay gave my neighbor the time he needed to exit his house and get halfway down his driveway before I could bend over and pick up the waste.

He looked about ten years older than me and was several inches shorter. I know it's shallow of me to point out those details to you, but hey, I'm still a bit perturbed by the incident. If he wants to give his side of things and make fun of my appearance, he can write his own damn story.

He threatened to injure me if he ever saw the dog on his lawn again. It was a serious overreaction, at least in my humble opinion. Maybe you feel differently.

I tried to be patient and just take the abuse, but then he threatened to shoot Maui, which was a major mistake. I told him if he ever threatened my dog again, I would, in fact, choke him out and not think twice about it. He informed me he was going to call the police and report the threat. I shamelessly encouraged him to do so and implied that I had serious connections with the Maui Police Department. All of this was over a tiny pile of poop from a ten-pound dog which was now in a plastic bag in my hand. I walked home and vented to Foxx about the incident. He laughed at first, but then he reminded me that the guy could have had a gun and that you can't protect yourself from crazy. I got the point.

I went for a long run on one of those afternoons. It was maybe six or seven miles. I replayed the search for Charlotte's secret in my mind. I saw myself going through each of the rooms in her house. I saw the letters hidden under the desk calendar. I saw the key with the storage unit number on it. I pictured the inside of her storage unit. I had found the letters from Edelman and the photographs in an old shoebox at the bottom of a stack of other boxes. Despite their presence in a room full of junk, I knew they had to mean something for her to have kept them all of these years, and she must have known she risked her family discovering the truth about Joe's paternity, if they didn't know already.

As I took a shower after the run, I thought about Trevor Edelman's attendance at Joe's funeral. His presence there had been a surprise to me. Joe's brother and sister hadn't come, so why had

Trevor? Especially after accusing the Chambers family of ripping off his family.

I climbed out of the shower and got dressed. I looked at my watch. It was just after five o'clock. I didn't know how late Trevor's boat-building company was open, and the website offered nothing more than a few photos of the boats and an email address for more information. It wasn't a long drive from Foxx's house, so I decided to go there anyway. I arrived in time to see Trevor's few employees pulling out of the parking lot. I parked near the main warehouse door, which was still open. I got out of my car and entered the building, but I didn't see Trevor.

I took a moment to walk around and admire the boats again. The craftsmanship was undeniable. Trevor and his team were truly gifted. There was no office in the warehouse, so I guessed Trevor might be out the back.

I exited the back door and found him sitting on the table under the tree where Alana and I had interviewed him before. He was drinking a beer, and he took a long gulp. I knew he saw me as soon as I walked outside because we made solid eye contact with each other, but he didn't say anything or even acknowledge my presence with a wave or nod. I walked over to him.

"It's good to see you again," I said. I wasn't sure how else to greet him. Trevor said nothing in response. "I was a little surprised to see you at Joe's funeral," I continued.

Trevor took another swig of his beer.

"Did you know Joe well?" I asked.

"Not well," he finally said.

"I only met him a couple of times myself."

"Why did you go to his funeral then?" Trevor asked.

"It seemed like the right thing to do, and I wasn't sure if his brother or sister were going to be there. I thought someone should be there."

"Those two are real assholes," he said.

I didn't know how to respond to his harsh words. It was a true statement, at least in regard to them not attending their own sibling's funeral.

"Do you mind me asking you a question about your father?"

"Depends what the question is," Trevor said.

"Why did he leave the Chambers Hotel?" I asked.

"I thought I told you that the last time you were here. He and Chambers had a falling out."

"I know, but what was it over?"

"It's been decades, man, and I was really young. I didn't know what was really going on."

"What about your mother? Would she know?" I asked.

"She's dead. She died when I was just a kid," Trevor said.

"I'm sorry to hear that."

I wasn't sure the best way to transition to the topic I really wanted to talk about. I think both Trevor and I knew the reason I'd come over, but we were both secretly hoping the other would be the person to bring it up first, or maybe the guy was desperately hoping I'd avoid the question. Unfortunately, Trevor didn't seem to be in a talkative mood. I considered stretching out the conversation a bit more, but then again, what would have been the point? He was either going to answer my question or he wasn't.

"You knew, didn't you? That was why you were at the funeral," I said.

"Knew what?" he asked.

"You just telling me your mother died adds another piece to why your father had a relationship with Charlotte. Maybe your father was vulnerable. Maybe he was looking for comfort. That certainly didn't make him a bad person. It made him human."

Trevor said nothing, which was really an answer unto itself. He didn't ask me what I was talking about, and he didn't tell me to go to hell.

"Did your father ever tell you, or did you figure it out on your own?" I asked.

Trevor hesitated some more. He took another drink of his beer.

He twisted the bottle around in his hands. He looked up at the tree branches that shaded him, and then he looked back at the bottle.

"She used to bring him around a lot when I was little. We would play together in the backyard. I remember doing that."

"I guess she didn't bring Mill and Bethany with her."

Trevor shook his head.

"My father would play with us both. He was always happy when she brought Joe around."

"When did you realize what was going on?" I asked.

"When I was a teenager. I don't remember exactly what year it was. I hadn't seen Joe in a few years. That may not make sense because this island is so small, but we went to different schools, and my father would do anything to avoid the Chambers family. When I finally saw Joe again, I was shocked."

"Why?" I asked.

"Because of how much he looked like my father," Trevor admitted.

"Did you ask your father about it?"

"Years later." Trevor laughed. "It took me that long to get up the courage, but he didn't admit it. He didn't deny it, either."

"What did he say?" I asked.

"He asked me if that was something Joe had told me. I told him it wasn't. I told him it was something I thought about on my own. He didn't say anything after that. He just walked out of the room."

"Did you ever ask him about it again?"

"No, I knew after that he would never tell me," Trevor said.

"Do you think that's the reason your father and Chambers broke up their partnership?"

"The timing would be about right." Trevor paused. Then he asked, "How did you figure this out?"

"Same way you did, really. The resemblance was uncanny."

"Yeah, but you didn't know what my father looked like."

"I found a photo of him with Charlotte Chambers in her house," I said.

I didn't want to tell him about my snooping through the storage unit, nor did I say anything about the love letters written by Edward Edelman. I wasn't sure how Trevor would feel about those, especially if they were written shortly after his mother's death. I also couldn't be totally sure of the timeline. They could have been written before his mother died.

"She really had a photo?" he asked.

I nodded. "It was hidden, of course. I found it while I was looking for evidence."

"Do you think Joe knew?" Trevor asked.

I thought back to a comment Candi had made to me. She said Mill and Bethany hated Joe from the moment he was born. She also said Joe had no idea why. Was that a lie Joe told Candi, or did he truly have no idea why they felt that way?

"His family treated him like an outcast, but I don't think he knew why, at least nothing he was willing to admit to anyone else," I said.

"Like I said before, they're assholes."

Again, I didn't know how to respond. What about Edward Edelman? Was he an asshole, too, for not acknowledging his son? Was it an agreement he made with Charlotte so her husband would raise the boy?

I thanked Trevor for his time and wished him good luck with the business. I knew this wasn't scientific proof yet, but between the photo, the love letters, and Trevor's story of confronting his father, this was about as close as I was going to get to confirmation that Joe Chambers was really Edward Edelman's son.

17

THE FUNERAL – PART 3

I SPENT ANOTHER WEEK NOT DOING MUCH OF ANYTHING REGARDING THE case. I walked the dog past that one neighbor's house once a day, but despite all of my urging to do so, Maui decided he had no desire to do his business there again.

Foxx and I got hooked on one of those cooking shows. The contestants had to make a dish out of raw peanuts, honey, creamed spinach, and some chicken that was actually black in color. The thing looked like it had already been cooked for days.

"What the hell are they going to do with that thing?" Foxx asked.

I didn't have an answer, so I just shrugged and finished my beer.

"I'm gonna get another one. You want one?" I asked.

"You have to ask?"

I climbed off the sofa and headed into the kitchen. Maui the dog followed me. I knew why. I kept a bag of his treats on the counter. I broke one in half and made him sit. He actually did it this time. He wagged his tail as I bent over to give him the Milk-Bone. I walked over to the refrigerator and pulled out three beers, one for me and two for Foxx.

I went back into the living room and handed Foxx his beers.

"Thanks," he said.

We watched the contestants hack away at the black chicken. The thing looked disgusting. Alana called me, though, before I could see them finish their meals for the judges.

"Hey there. How's it going?" I asked.

"Tell her about the black chicken," Foxx said.

Before I could tell her, Alana said, "Can you come to Bethany's house?"

"What's going on?" I asked.

"There's been another death."

Alana ended the call before I could say another word. It was a long drive to Bethany's, and the traffic was terrible. I wanted to call Alana back multiple times, but I knew she'd have her hands full.

I had been to crime scenes before, and this one was no different. There were several police cars in front of the house. An ambulance was also there. The back of the emergency vehicle was open, and there wasn't a stretcher inside. It must have been taken into the house.

I parked several houses down from Bethany's and texted Alana. I then walked as close as I could to Bethany's house. A police officer eventually came out of the house and approached me.

"Your name Poe?" he asked.

"Yes."

"Come with me."

He escorted me past the crowd and to the front door.

"Wait here," he ordered.

I stood on the porch for several more minutes. I was about to text Alana again when the emergency medical technicians brought a body out on the stretcher. The body was covered with a sheet, so I wasn't able to tell who it was. I guessed it had to be Bethany or Barry. I watched them cart the body down the driveway and lift the stretcher into the back of the ambulance. They shut the doors and climbed into the front but didn't immediately drive away. I waited a few more minutes before Alana came to the door.

"Hey," she said.

"Bethany?" I asked.

Alana nodded. She led me inside. I looked around but didn't see Barry. I followed Alana to the master bedroom. I noticed the covers on the bed were slightly disturbed, like someone had been lying on top of the covers but not underneath them.

"Did you find her on the bed?" I asked.

"Yes, she was on her back."

Alana motioned to the nightstand. "There was a note," she added.

I looked at the nightstand and saw a white piece of paper on top of it. I walked over and read the two words which were handwritten, at the very top: "I'm sorry."

"Suicide?" I asked.

"Maybe."

"Is she saying she's sorry for killing herself? What if she's apologizing for something else she did?" I asked.

"Like killing her mother?"

"Was the cause of death obvious?" I asked.

"Pills, I'm guessing."

I followed Alana's gaze back to the nightstand where I saw an empty prescription bottle alongside an empty glass. Alana turned to me.

"There were no visible signs of trauma."

I'd noticed the lack of blood on the bed and carpet as soon as I'd entered the room.

I bent closer to the empty pill bottle. Her name was on the label along with the name of the drug, Estazolam.

"Were these sleeping pills?" I asked.

"Yes, I looked the prescription up on my phone."

"Fingerprints?" I asked.

"We dusted for them but need to compare them to Bethany's."

"Where's Barry?" I asked.

"He's on Oahu at some marketing conference. He's catching the first flight back tonight."

"How did he take it?"

"Quietly. He didn't say much. I think he's in shock," Alana said.

"What about the daughter, Olivia?" I asked.

"We don't have a number for her. Barry said he'd call her."

"I know the place where she works, if that would help."

"Maybe. I'll let you know."

I looked around the room. Nothing seemed disturbed beyond the bed cover. I saw a cedar chest. The drawers were still in place. The photographs on top of the chest were still standing. There was a television sitting on a black table. The TV was off, and the remote control was on the table. I examined the other nightstand on the opposite side of the bed. There was a paperback on it and a digital clock with glowing blue numbers. I studied a painting on the wall. It was of a rocky shoreline with green-covered mountains, an iconic image of the island of Kauai. I turned back to Alana.

"There's one more thing. I found a nine-millimeter handgun in the other nightstand. The safety is on, but it's loaded with a full magazine," Alana said.

"Understandable. Would you want to off yourself with a gun or a bottle of sleeping pills?" I asked.

"Yeah, but that's not what I was getting at. The gun has no prints on it, at least on the handle. There are, however, prints on the magazine."

"Okay, that's interesting. Did someone point the gun at her and force her to write the note and take the pills?" I asked.

"The thought crossed my mind. We'll have to compare the prints on the magazine to Barry's. I'm guessing they're his."

"What does your gut say?" I asked.

"I don't know. I just don't know." She paused a moment and then asked, "Yours?"

"Same here," I said.

"Barry's flight should arrive in a couple of hours. I've asked him to come to the station."

I nodded. I knew that was also her way of telling me I wasn't going to be part of the interview process. I was actually surprised she'd called me to Bethany's house. I figured she was tight with the other officers present, but I didn't know if any of them would casually mention my presence to the captain. I knew she'd take some serious heat after he'd told her to take me off the investigation.

"There's something else. I already got a call from Mara Winters. She's going to be there with him," Alana said.

"Tonight?" I asked.

"Yeah."

"His wife just died, maybe committed suicide, and the first thing he thought to do was call his lawyer?" I asked.

"I know what you mean. It's exactly what I was thinking, too. I'll give you a call as soon as it's over."

I thanked Alana for keeping me in the loop as much as possible. I left the house and drove back to Foxx's. The traffic was still bad, so I had plenty of time to think about what I had just seen and heard. It made no sense that Barry would immediately call Mara. He had a solid alibi for the time of Bethany's death. I don't even think anyone would have considered him for the perpetrator anyway. But what about that gun? I knew people routinely cleaned their weapons, at least I thought they were supposed to do that. Is that how the prints got wiped off the handle of the gun? Probably not. But did that mean Bethany's death had to be murder?

Foxx was still watching the cooking show on television by the time I got back. They must have been having some marathon on that particular channel. I told him about Bethany's death, Barry calling his attorney, and the note with the two-word message.

"The dude lawyered up fast, didn't he?" Foxx said.

"You had the same reaction we did," I said.

"Who wouldn't? You'd think all he'd care about was finding out who did this, if it was even murder, that is," Foxx said.

I thought about Olivia and wondered if she'd be at the station with her father. How would she respond when she saw his cold reaction? Or was it even cold? Was I being unfair by judging him? I'd never been married before, but I loved Alana deeply. I had no idea how I'd truly react if she died suddenly. Maybe I'd go into shock, too, and act in a strange way.

I watched the television show for a few minutes and then got up to walk the dog. I just couldn't sit still. I really wanted to be at the police station and see Barry for myself, but I knew that was impossible. I got back to the house and gave the dog a treat. I grabbed a beer out of the refrigerator and walked outside to the pool. The night air was cool. I sat beside the pool for a couple of hours and listened to the ocean waves hitting the rock jetty behind Foxx's house. He owned one of the most beautiful pieces of property on the island. I knew I couldn't live with my friend forever, and I also knew I would truly miss this place once I eventually left.

I finally went back inside the house and walked to my bedroom. I sat on the bed and turned on the television. Believe it or not, that cooking competition show was still going. I watched it for all of sixty seconds before I switched it off. I lay on my back for a few minutes and then rolled over to my side. I looked down at the floor and saw Maui the dog sleeping. His tiny chest rose and fell as he breathed in and out. Then I heard my cell phone vibrate on the nightstand. I looked at the clock beside it. It was almost eleven o'clock.

"Hello," I said.

"It's me," Alana said.

"You okay?" I asked. Her voice sounded rough.

"Yeah, just beyond exhausted. I'm still at the office, believe it or not."

"I believe it," I said. "How did it go with Barry?"

"It was a complete waste of time. I got next to nothing out of him. He's been at the marketing conference in Honolulu for the last week. Bethany didn't go because she wasn't feeling well. He showed me a hotel receipt to prove he was there. He also showed me his boarding passes, both for the flight out there and the return flight."

"The guy came prepared. I guess he thought you were going to try to pin this on him," I said.

"I assume so, but I don't know why. I never even hinted at it."

"What did Mara say?" I asked.

"Not much. Once she realized we weren't going to charge him, she stayed pretty quiet."

"Did you ask him if he thought it might be suicide?"

"Of course. He said his wife had been depressed about her mother's and brother's deaths, but he never thought she'd want to take her own life."

"Interesting that he would make a point to bring up Joe, considering neither he nor Bethany were at the funeral," I said.

"Exactly. Makes you wonder how upset she really was," Alana said.

"I'm guessing it was an act, at least the Joe part. It wouldn't look good to say she hadn't cared a damn about him. What about the pills?"

"Their family doctor recently prescribed them. Barry said Bethany was having trouble sleeping after Charlotte died."

"What about the note?" I asked.

"He wasn't sure what she was referring to, either."

"And Olivia? Was she there?"

"She showed up right as we were finishing with Barry. Mara stayed for her interview as well."

"How did she appear?" I asked.

"She cried, not sobs, mind you, but she definitely reacted more than her father did. She also said she didn't know her mother was depressed enough to take her own life, but neither of them had any idea who would want to hurt her."

Alana and I spoke for a few more minutes. There really wasn't much she had to go on at that point. A murder or a suicide? It was anyone's guess.

The autopsy was done the next day. The medical examiner confirmed what Alana already suspected. Death was caused by Bethany swallowing a large dose of Estazolam.

Alana had the fingerprints on the glass compared to Bethany's. They matched, and there were no other fingerprints on it. The fingerprints on the ammunition clip matched Barry. He told Alana that he didn't remember the last time he cleaned the weapon, and it didn't make sense to him that there were no fingerprints on the handle as well. He also told her that he and Bethany used to fight over him having the gun in the house, especially in the bedroom where they slept. He said she was terribly afraid of guns and didn't see any reason for them to have one since they lived in a nice neighborhood.

The police had a cause of death but still no answers.

All Alana and I really knew for sure was that of the four immediate members of the Chambers family that had been alive when I first got this assignment from Mara, three were now gone. I thought about Charlotte's original will. Did the death of Joe and Bethany mean everything would go to Mill? I didn't know if the will had even been entered into probate. For that matter, I wasn't even sure if Joe's fake will had actually been declared fake. Money might be a trivial concern when one compares it to the importance of a human life, but there were millions of dollars at stake, and I didn't know if that had anything to do with Bethany's death.

I went to Bethany's funeral. The same minister who officiated Charlotte's and Joe's funerals was there. He continued his paint-by-numbers approach when describing Bethany's life and how much she would be missed by friends and family. He listed her numerous accolades. Among them, Bethany had been a successful marketing manager for one of the top hotels on Maui. Not according to her mother-in-law, I thought, but no one wants to tell the truth about someone at her funeral. *She was a mediocre employee, and she wasn't particularly nice to others.* Yeah, that would never fly, but it sure would make these things more entertaining.

Unlike the days of the previous two funerals, the weather was threatening to rain. The sky was a dark gray, and the air felt oppressive and sticky. I'd broken out the dark suit for a third time this month. I'd definitely have to get it dry cleaned again.

Mill and his wife, Jen, attended the funeral. Apparently, their boycotting of funerals only extended to Joe Chambers. I didn't see their twin sons, and I found their lack of attendance tacky at best. It's an easy flight from San Francisco to Maui. Were they really that busy?

Barry and Olivia sat in the front row, just a few feet from the casket. Barry's face looked like stone. I couldn't tell if he was angry, sad, dismayed, depressed, all of the above, or none of the above.

Olivia was beside him. She held a handkerchief and kept dabbing it at the corners of her moist eyes.

The overall attendance was much higher than the funeral for Joe, but there were far less people than the one for Charlotte. I was told there would be no wake after the service. The family, apparently, wanted to be alone.

The rain finally started to come down. At first, it was more of a sprinkle. The minister sped up his service, but we were all still drenched when the rain clouds fully opened toward the end. Everyone, except Barry, scattered for their cars. I also walked back to my car but didn't drive away. Instead, I sat there and watched Barry. He never left his seat in the front row, despite the heavy rain.

Olivia had driven separately, which I found a bit odd. I knew from previous funerals I had attended where a family member had died that the families tended to pile together in one or two cars. Sometimes a limousine or town car was even rented, but Olivia apparently had driven herself, as had her father. Did that mean anything? I wasn't sure.

I drove around the cemetery and picked a spot where I could see Barry's car in the distance. Hopefully, he wouldn't notice mine. The rain continued to fall hard for at least another hour. Barry still hadn't left his seat by the casket. Finally, after the rain let up and the clouds started to part, I saw Barry stand and walk to his car. He climbed inside and drove off.

I couldn't begin to imagine his misery. His wife was gone. All of their plans were gone, too. I'm sure he didn't know what he'd do or how he'd move forward with his life. And what about Olivia? How would this tragic loss alter her course?

I drove back to Bethany's gravesite and parked my car. I got out and walked up to the temporary grave marker. It was several feet from Charlotte's. I walked over to her gravestone. She and Millard Chambers shared one of those larger stones that had both of their names on it. The last name, Chambers, was large and at the top and center of the marker. Millard's name and dates of birth and death were on the left side, and Charlotte's on the right. I walked another several feet and saw Joe's gravestone. Despite him feeling like an outcast, he was now fated to lie beside the rest of the clan for eternity.

I thought back to Joe's funeral and seeing Trevor Edelman there. He hadn't come to Bethany's, which was certainly no surprise. I'd watched Trevor walk away and head across the cemetery after Joe's service. Trevor had stopped at a particular gravestone, but I was too far away from him to read it.

I headed in the same direction. I remembered the gravestone he'd looked at was close to a tree. I found that tree easily enough, but it took me several more minutes of looking at various graves before I found one with the name Edward Edelman on it. I looked at the two gravestones on each side of Edward's. They belonged to men, but they had different last names, definitely not brothers or a father to Edelman. Maybe they were cousins from an aunt who married and took another last name. Maybe they were strangers.

I then noticed that Edward Edelman's gravestone didn't have the name of his wife. Trevor said she had died when he was a small child. I'd have thought she and her husband would have been buried together. I walked around and looked for her gravestone. I couldn't find her name anywhere. In fact, I couldn't find any other marker with the last name of Edelman. Edward, it seemed, was all alone.

I called Alana and checked in with her. They'd made no progress on Bethany's case beyond what I'd detailed to you earlier, and she said she thought the district attorney was probably going to rule it a suicide. There just wasn't any evidence to support murder. Bethany's fingerprints were the only ones in the room, except for Barry's on the odd item like the paperback, the television remote, and some of the metal handles on the cedar chest. The nine-millimeter belonged to Barry, but he was on another island when the death occurred.

The next day I couldn't stop thinking about Edward Edelman's gravesite. I know that may sound strange. I just didn't understand why I hadn't been able to find Trevor's mother's grave. I realized, too, that I didn't even know her first name. I wanted to ask Trevor about it, but I knew I'd be crossing a line and come across as a borderline stalker of the Edelman family. Maybe I was. I'd be lying to you if I didn't admit I was a bit freaked out by my own curiosity.

I did multiple Google searches for Edelman, combining it with keywords, such as *Hawaii, Maui, Chambers Hotel,* and *Millard Chambers*. Not much turned up, and there was no mention of Edward's wife in any of the searches.

I decided to search for Edward Edelman's marriage license or Trevor Edelman's birth certificate. The birth certificate seemed like it would be way harder to get. The few websites I found required you to order the birth certificate after entering your personal information, so I spent most of my energy on the marriage license.

I went to the local library and asked if they had digital copies of old issues of the local paper. Their digital records didn't go back very far, but they suggested I go to the city clerk's office. Again, the rare name of Edelman worked in my favor, as did my slipping one of the clerks a hundred bucks to help me out. The clerk told me he viewed it as a personal challenge to find such an old marriage license, and he'd recently forgotten his wife's birthday. He was going to use my money to take her out to a nice restaurant and hopefully get out of the proverbial dog house. The clerk was able to eventually find a scanned copy of the license. The wife's name had been Rebecca Acker.

I thanked the clerk profusely and went home to do a Google search on Rebecca Edelman. I got nothing, though, so I tried Rebecca Acker, along with the word *Hawaii*. That was when everything changed.

I clicked on the top hit; it was a link to an article in the *Honolulu Star Advisor*. According to the article, a Ms. Rebecca Acker recently donated one million dollars to renovate an arts center on Oahu. The center had been founded twenty years before and was dedicated to promoting the art and culture of the native Hawaiian people. There was also a color photograph of Ms. Acker. Judging by her appearance, she was old enough to be the mother of Trevor Edelman.

I hit the back button on the browser and reviewed the other hits from my search. I spent the next hour going through most of them.

There were no references to Edward Edelman or Trevor Edelman, but there were plenty of articles about the philanthropy of the Acker family. From what I could gather, they made their fortune in farming sugar cane.

I ended my Internet session and walked outside to the pool to get some fresh air and soak my feet in the warm water. Was it possible that the Rebecca Acker I found on the Internet was the same person who married Edward Edelman? If so, why would Trevor lie about his mother being dead when she was very much alive on Oahu?

18

PATRICIA

A MONTH PASSED. I DIDN'T DO ANYTHING WITH THE KNOWLEDGE THAT Trevor Edelman had lied to me. I guess I could have confronted him about it, but what would have been the point? I did tell Alana about the discovery that Rebecca Acker was still alive. She also couldn't come up with a reason Trevor had hidden the truth. I did my best to forget about it, but there was something about the bizarre little mystery that made it keep popping up in my mind from time to time. Then I'd think about it for a few more minutes and tell myself to drop it again.

The cold case of Charlotte Chambers' murder had officially frozen. In my imagination, which is often too vivid, I saw Alana placing the Charlotte Chambers' files into a proverbial cardboard box and then carting it into a government warehouse where it would collect dust and never be opened again. It made me sick to think the killer had gotten away with it. I still remembered the sight of Charlotte floating in her swimming pool. I'd turned the backyard lights on and saw the blood swirling and twirling around her lifeless body.

Alana and I had fallen back into our normal routine. I did my thing during the day, such as it was, and we'd meet up sometime after her shift ended. We spent about half the week at her house and the other half at Foxx's. I guess you could say we were in the comfort zone as far as relationships go.

There wasn't much more to report regarding Foxx and Hani. Foxx still refused to talk about her. I shouldn't really say he refused. It wasn't like I asked him questions, and he told me to get lost. He just never brought her up, and I didn't either. I actually only saw Hani once that month. She showed up at Alana's house when I was over. We spoke for a couple of hours, and then she left. She hadn't brought up Foxx either. I asked Alana if she knew anything, and she said she didn't. I admitted that I didn't know anything either.

One afternoon, Alana called me and invited me for sushi at her favorite place which happened to be near her office and the airport. I was actually pretty bored, so I decided to head over to Harry's first, which was on the way to the sushi place. I was fairly surprised to see Patricia, Charlotte's assistant, when I entered the bar. She was sitting in a corner booth by herself. I walked over to say hello.

"Hey there," I said. "I thought you were moving back to California."

I'd made the comment right as she took a large bite of her hamburger. She held up one finger.

"Sorry. Yeah, that was the plan, but I ended up getting a job offer and decided to stay on Maui," she said.

"Oh, where are you working now?" I asked.

"With Olivia Williams at her wedding planning company. I met her at the funeral, and we got to talking about her business. She said she was really getting busy and had thought about hiring someone to help out."

"How are things going there?"

"Good. Really good. The business has taken off. She's already talking about maybe bringing on a third person."

"You must stay really busy then," I said.

"Totally. I barely have time to eat. Her office is just a few blocks from here. If I'm lucky, I can just squeeze in a tight run over here. I usually call ahead, so they can have the food ready by the time I get here."

"That's smart. When you see Olivia again, please tell her I said thanks again for the advice she gave me."

"Are you planning a wedding?" Patricia asked.

"Not exactly. I asked her for recommendations on a jeweler. She gave me the name of a guy, but I haven't had a chance to see him yet."

"I'll let her know."

"Did you know Olivia before Charlotte's funeral?" I asked.

"No, she never came over to the house, at least not when I was there, but I wasn't at Charlotte's day and night."

"I still can't believe she's gone," I said.

"It's so sad," Patricia said.

"Well, I'll leave you to your lunch, or is it dinner?"

Patricia looked at the time on her cell phone.

"I guess I'm somewhere in between."

"Take care, and please tell Olivia I said hello."

"I will."

I walked over to the bar and ordered a beer. I could see Patricia's reflection in the mirror behind the bar, so I saw her when she stood and waved goodbye to me. I turned around and waved back. I finished my beer and paid the tab.

I was a little early meeting Alana at the sushi restaurant, a lot early, actually. I parked the car and walked under a tree near the parking lot to get some shade. I pulled out my cell phone and logged onto Facebook. I had an account but hardly ever used it. I typed Patricia's name into the search bar and found her account. She hadn't turned on the privacy settings. I searched through her contacts and discovered she was listed as a friend of Olivia Williams, not surprising considering they now worked together. I then clicked on Patricia's photos and saw she had over a thousand. I closed the web page and slipped the phone back into my pocket. I wasn't about to attempt to go through that many photos on my phone while sitting under a tree.

I thought about my conversation with Patricia. Did I find it realistic that she'd never met Olivia before the funeral? Maybe. Olivia had told me she hadn't seen her family much since starting the wedding company. I'd never run my own company before, but I guessed it was extremely time consuming, especially if she was the only employee. Maybe she only saw her grandmother on the occasional weekend, and maybe Patricia didn't work weekends.

Alana arrived, and we went inside to have an early dinner. I told her about bumping into Patricia at the bar. I then told her I'd been questioning whether or not Patricia had met Olivia before the funeral.

"Why would she lie about that?" Alana asked.

"I don't know. It's just one of those things that seems weird to me."

Alana just shrugged her shoulders and picked up a California roll with her chopsticks. I wasn't sure if she found my obsession with details that seemed rather insignificant charming or annoying. Maybe it was neither. Maybe it was one of those quirks that you put up with if you want to be in a relationship with someone. So what are her quirks that I put up with? You don't really expect me to answer that, do you?

We finished dinner, and she followed me back to Foxx's because she said she had the urge to swim in the pool. Alana had left a couple of swimsuits at the house, but she ended up not needing one. Foxx called me on the way home to check in. I think he was a bit concerned with my mental state because I'd not yet been able to help Alana solve the Chambers' murder. He knew I'd been stressed about it, probably even downright depressed. Perhaps my attitude and temperament had been even worse than I realized. I told him I was okay and informed him that Alana and I were heading to the house to enjoy the pool. He told me to tell her hello and let me know he would be out for the night. Was he going to see Hani? Again, I didn't ask.

We got back to Foxx's place and decided to swim in the nude since we were alone. The water temperature was perfect, as it usually was. Alana asked if I wanted to watch television after the swim. I guess it was one of those things couples do when they're in the comfort zone I referenced earlier, but then I got a good glimpse of her climbing out of the pool, and I told her we'd need to postpone the television for later that night. I climbed out after her and picked her up. She laughed and asked if I was doing my caveman routine. I told her I was and carried her into the bedroom where we made love. I don't recall deciding to fall asleep afterward. It just sort of happened, as it tends to with males.

I woke up in the middle of the night when I heard Maui the dog whining. I looked down to the floor and saw him sitting at the edge of the bed and looking up at me. I hadn't taken the dog for his usual nightly walk since I'd spent that time in the pool and then the bedroom. The poor guy probably had his legs crossed most of the night.

I climbed out of bed, and he followed me to the back of the house. I opened the sliding glass door, and he darted outside. I thought about immediately going to bed, but then I saw my laptop on the kitchen table. I don't know why I decided to do this in the middle of the night. Maybe it's that obsession thing I mentioned before, but I logged onto Facebook and started searching through Patricia's photographs. It took me a couple of hours, and Alana came into the room just as I found what I was really looking for.

"It's six o'clock. How long have you been up?" Maui the dog ran up to her. "Good morning, Maui," she said, and she bent down and scratched him behind his ears.

"I'm not exactly sure when I got up, but take a look at this."

Alana walked over to the kitchen table, and I turned the laptop around so she could see the screen.

"What am I looking at?" she asked.

"Patricia's photos on her Facebook account. Check out who's in the background of that shot."

Alana leaned closer to the screen.

"Which person?" she asked.

The shot was one of those behind-the-scenes group photos you sometimes see from video production crews. After going through her Facebook albums, I learned that about half of her photos were these types of shots. Patricia had apparently worked in the film industry in Los Angeles.

"It's Olivia Williams. Olivia told me she used to work in commercials and music videos. It turns out Patricia did, too. There are several shots of Olivia throughout Patricia's photo albums," I said.

"You think she knew Olivia?" Alana asked.

"I realize there are a ton of production people and actors in L. A. Hell, probably every other person in that city is somehow related to that business, but I find it hard to believe Patricia wouldn't have known Olivia if they worked on several productions together."

"Then Patricia moves to Maui about the same time Olivia moves back and ends up working for Olivia's grandmother," Alana said.

"Exactly. There are coincidences, but that one is ridiculous."

"Olivia must have gotten her the job with Charlotte."

"That makes sense, so why lie about not meeting Olivia until the funeral?" I asked.

"It's strange," Alana admitted. "You were up all night looking at these photos, weren't you?"

"Not all night. Maybe only half."

Alana looked at the Facebook photo again.

"Yeah, she had to have known Olivia," Alana said.

"So what do we do with this information?" I asked.

"I don't know. All it proves is that Patricia lied to you about Olivia and nothing more."

I looked at the laptop screen. Yeah, she lied all right, but why?

19

REBECCA ACKER

THERE WAS SOMETHING ABOUT SEEING PATRICIA AND DISCOVERING she'd lied to me that reignited my passion for solving the case. Oh, who am I kidding? It wasn't like my passion and determination had gone away. I just didn't know where to look, and I had allowed myself to fall into a funk. I still didn't know how to break this thing open, but I decided it needed to be approached as if I were looking for lost car keys. I just needed to start turning over anything I could find and hoping there would be something underneath.

I thought about Charlotte Chambers. She was not the person I initially thought she was. Of course, my opinion of her was nothing short of superficial, so it really wasn't much of a surprise when she turned out to be different than I'd imagined. There were mysteries about the woman as evidenced by my discovery in the storage unit. She also lied about destroying the threatening letters. Why? What about the two letters I found in her home office? They said she wasn't innocent and questioned who the real monster was. Were those letters in addition to the ones she told me about in Mara's office? Or were they the original two letters and she didn't want me to know someone had alluded to her guilt of doing something bad? It had to be bad, too. You don't get called a monster if you fail to pay your parking tickets.

It was obvious there were things she didn't want me to know. She probably didn't think I needed to know them at the time. I understood that. Nobody wants to tell someone their secrets, especially some guy you've just met at your lawyer's office. She was desperate and scared. So what was the secret that Charlotte had wanted to stay buried, and who could possibly tell me?

I knew I'd never get anything out of the remaining members of the Chambers family. Maybe they didn't even know the secret, or secrets. There was one person, however, who might.

I decided to start with Rebecca Acker. Why had Trevor told me she was dead? It was time to find out, or at least try to find out. I called the Acker Foundation and attempted to set up an appointment to see Rebecca. I was told she generally didn't accept meetings anymore, and that I was better off seeing the current director of the foundation. I called a second time and told them to please relay to Rebecca that it was a matter regarding her son. They got back to me later that day and scheduled an appointment for the following day.

I booked a flight for Oahu. I didn't tell Alana what I was doing. She'd have thought I was crazy. The flight from Maui is pretty quick, as I'm sure you can imagine. It actually took me way longer to drive the rental car from the airport to Honolulu, where the Acker Foundation was located. I know I sometimes complain about the traffic on Maui, but it's nothing compared to Oahu. Honolulu is traditionally listed as one of the top five worst cities for traffic. I think Los Angeles and Washington D.C. are a couple of places that always beat it.

The Acker Foundation was in a small but impressive building. It was made of huge panels of glass and thick beams of polished metal. Large palm trees surrounded it. There were even huge tropical plants and smaller trees inside the lobby. I guessed they were able to thrive inside since the building resembled a greenhouse.

I waited in the lobby for close to an hour. I didn't know if the lady was just busy or if this was some sort of strange power play. Eventually, a young woman, maybe only twenty, came out and led me back to Rebecca's office. The office also consisted of glass and metal. The back wall was entirely glass, and there were so many thick tropical plants on the outside that it looked like the building was backed up to a rainforest. I sat in her office for another half an hour before she showed. Yeah, this had to be a power play.

I stood when she finally arrived. In a way, she reminded me of Charlotte Chambers. She was about the same age, and she had that air of confidence and resolve that Charlotte had possessed. She didn't shake my hand, but instead, she walked right past me and around to the opposite side of her desk and sat down. I sat back down on the chair in front of her. I wouldn't be surprised if the lady had had my chair lowered a few inches just to further increase her psychological edge.

"So, Mr. Rutherford, how much money are you here to ask for?"

"I'm not sure I understand," I said.

"Your message said this was about my son. So how much do you and he want?"

"Trevor doesn't know I'm here, and I don't want any of your money."

I thought about yelling "Take that!" when I saw the look on her face. I won't say I'd gained the upper hand. In fact, I wasn't even sure there was an upper hand to be gained, but I could tell she'd just gone from being certain she knew what this was all about to being incredibly off-balance. I sensed it wasn't a position she normally found herself in.

"Then what is it you want?" she asked.

"Trevor told me you were dead," I said, hoping to further throw her off.

"I'm not surprised."

I told her how I'd recently been to the cemetery and saw the gravesite of her husband, Edward Edelman, and how the absence of her name on the gravestone was my first clue that not everything was as it seemed.

"Edward wasn't my husband. Well, he was at one point, but he was my ex by the time he died."

"Are you aware of all that's going on with the Chambers family? The media on Maui is having a field day, but I'm not sure if that interest transfers over here. I'm rather new to Hawaii, and I must admit I don't have a good sense for how connected the islands really are."

"Charlotte's murder made the news here. And I'm aware that two of her children died, but I try not to think about that family. What is your interest in them?" she asked.

I gave Rebecca the short version of my involvement, starting with my initial meeting with Charlotte and then making my way to Joe's drug overdose and Bethany's suicide, if you wanted to call it that.

"So you're a private investigator and not with the police?" she asked.

"That's right."

Rebecca hesitated, and I could tell she was debating whether to toss me out of her office, but she didn't. I wasn't sure why, exactly. Perhaps I'd piqued her curiosity.

"I thought you'd come here to tell me that you and my son were starting a new business. I thought you were going to ask me for money."

"I assume you've funded some of his start-ups before," I said.

"More than I can remember. They've all failed miserably."

Is there another way to fail? I asked myself.

"Did you also fund his boat-building company?" I asked.

"Yes."

"How long ago was that?"

"About two years ago."

"I saw the business when I met with him. He does beautiful work, for what it's worth."

"It's worth nothing. That's the problem. Who's going to spend money to buy a boat that looks like an ancient Hawaiian canoe?" she asked.

"You may be right. From what I could see, there weren't exactly a lot of customers beating down the door."

"There never are with my son."

"Do you stay in contact with Trevor?"

"No, the last time I spoke with him was when he asked for the money for the new company."

"Do you know why he would have told me you were deceased?" I asked.

"Trevor hates me. He thinks I ruined his and Eddie's lives when I left. Trevor's a grown man now, but he still can't let go of the past."

"Were you married to Edward Edelman when he was involved with the Chambers Hotel?"

"Are you kidding? I gave him the money to build that hotel. My family owned the land the hotel was built on."

"Did you have any involvement with the hotel beyond that?" I asked.

"Not really. I wanted Eddie to be successful on his own. We'd met in college. He had a lot of ambition. He knew I came from money, but he seemed determined to forge his own path, which I admired. We got married, and I had Trevor not long afterward. My father wasn't too keen about it all, but I was young and in love, so I didn't listen. It was the biggest mistake of my life."

"Why was your father against the marriage?" I asked.

"My father was an uneducated man, but he had the kind of smarts that only hard knocks can give you. He was the one who built the family fortune. He recognized Eddie for what he really was."

"Which was?"

"Someone who had the ambition but not the know-how and certainly not the drive to stick it out when the going got tough," she said.

"Since you weren't involved with the day-to-day running of the hotel, how well did you know the Chambers family?"

Rebecca scoffed. "Well enough."

I waited for Rebecca to elaborate but she didn't, at least not immediately. I studied her eyes closely. This may not make a lot of sense, but I thought I could see through them, all the way to the thoughts that were furiously running through her mind. She knew something, and it was big. I was certain of that now. I just didn't know if she'd share it with me.

"Charlotte described her husband, Millard, as a brilliant man. Was that a fair assessment?" I asked.

"Millard didn't have a lot of good qualities. What he did have was a sense of survival, much like a cockroach."

"Why did your husband have a falling out with him?" I asked.

"Why do any two people have a falling out? It's never one thing," she said.

"True, but usually there's a tipping point, the proverbial straw that broke the camel's back."

Rebecca didn't reply.

I paused a moment and then said, "I know about Joe Chambers. I'm sorry if that's a sensitive topic."

"It still hurts, even after all of these years," she said.

"I assume that was why you left Edward and why his business partnership with Millard fell apart."

"Our marriage was already over by that point. Eddie wasn't the man I thought he was, and I had lost interest in him quickly. I won't say I drove him to Charlotte. We were still married, and he shouldn't have cheated on me, but I wasn't exactly giving him what he needed. He wanted to be wanted. Adored, actually. I wasn't willing to do that. I couldn't and wouldn't fake how I felt."

"When I first met with Charlotte, she told me she'd received letters in the mail that threatened her life. She also told me she burned them, but I found them in her home office. They weren't threats, not exactly. They seemed to point to Charlotte's role in something. I don't know what it was, but they described her as a monster and not being innocent."

"I'm sure the Chambers family can tell you. It's not exactly a secret among them."

"The Chambers family isn't talking, and I want to figure out who killed Charlotte."

"What does it matter? The woman is gone," she said.

"I'm not sure how you can say that. Whatever she did, she was still human. She deserves justice."

"Justice? We all deserve justice, Mr. Rutherford. That doesn't mean we're going to get it, and I'd debate your statement that Charlotte was human."

"What happened? I know you know," I said.

"Charlotte was not innocent. She was only interested in maintaining her lifestyle. That's why she went back to him."

"To who? To Millard?"

"I'll give her this. She figured out Eddie way faster than I did. Once she realized the money came from me and not Eddie, she dropped him."

"Did your ex-husband lead people to believe you weren't behind the funding of the hotel?" I asked.

"I don't think he ever lied about it and denied I was the source of the funds. He just never brought it up. It's a man's world. It was back then, anyhow. People just assumed the money was from Eddie. They assumed he was the self-made man. Do you know how many businesses my ex tried to start after the Chambers Hotel? Even more than Trevor. They were all failures too, just like Trevor's. Unfortunately, Trevor inherited his father's knack for business."

"The affair and the birth of Joe Chambers...is that why Charlotte isn't innocent?"

"Joe has nothing to do with this. He never did. You've been looking at the wrong Chambers if you've been concentrating on him."

"Who should I be looking at?" I asked.

"The girl. I don't even remember her name anymore."

"Bethany."

Rebecca nodded. "Yes, that's it."

"What is it about Bethany?" I asked.

Rebecca said nothing. It felt like a full minute went by with neither of us saying a word. I tried to get her talking by asking another question.

"You said earlier that Millard was not a man of good qualities. What did you mean by that?"

"Oh, he knew how to run the hotel, and he certainly knew how to bully Eddie. He got what he wanted in the end. He got the property, the business, and his wife back. I guess you could say he won. Where's that justice you were talking about before?" she asked.

"What did he do that deserved justice?"

"Charlotte was devastated, as she had every right to be. She went running to Eddie, and of course, he was there to comfort her. One thing led to another, and they started their affair. I found out about it. They weren't exactly discreet, so I left him. They continued their affair afterward. I don't know for how long because I moved back with my family here on Oahu. Charlotte got pregnant with Joe. Maybe she was already pregnant while I was still married to Eddie. I'm not sure."

"You didn't stay in touch with your husband, even though you shared a son?" I asked.

"Trevor came with me to Oahu. I wasn't about to leave him with Eddie and Charlotte. He'd spend the summer months with his father on Maui. He eventually moved back there when he was a teenager."

"Why?"

"Typical parent-teenager stuff. I was hard on him. I'll admit that, but I wanted him to make something out of himself. I actually intended him to take over the Acker family business at one point, but the kid was lazy. He never wanted to do anything. I guess he moved back to Maui because he assumed things would be easier with his father."

"How long did Charlotte stay with Eddie?" I asked.

"Not long. She was still pregnant when she went back to Millard. It was a hell of a scandal, but it's long forgotten now. Charlotte was a survivor, too. She came from nothing, and she didn't want to go back to nothing. She was still with Eddie when he left the Chambers Hotel. I think she thought he would fight for it, but he didn't. He told me years later he just wanted to be rid of Millard and start a new life with Charlotte. Once Charlotte realized Eddie was broke and not likely to provide her with the life she wanted, she asked Millard to take her back."

"Why would Millard take her back, especially if it was already a scandal?" I asked.

"Because there was a bigger scandal on the horizon. Politicians do it all the time. They let one secret leak, so everyone goes crazy over it while the real dirt stays hidden. I'm certain she threatened to go to the police, too. Millard would have been ruined forever. They both got what they needed. Millard stayed out of jail and Charlotte got to be the big shot wife of a wealthy hotel owner. I saw in the news they're about to sell that place to a large chain of hotels. That family will make millions, and to think it all started with my father simply giving them that piece of land because I begged him to."

I thought back to the notes Charlotte received. "You aren't innocent. Who is the real monster? You know how this ends." They had to be related to the "real dirt" Rebecca just mentioned.

"What did Millard do?" I asked.

I wasn't sure I really wanted to know the answer, but Rebecca told me, and it made me sick.

I barely made it back to the airport in time to catch the early afternoon flight back to Maui. When I exited the airport in Kahului, I found myself walking to the rental car lot instead of the short-term parking area where I'd left my convertible. I remembered my lesson from the earlier case of following Doctor Peterson, and I rented the most boring sedan I could find. I even asked for a beige one. I know that wasn't the official color. They always have a fancier name like "desert sand," but this thing looked beige as far as I was concerned.

I drove to Lahaina and went to Harry's. It was still too early for Patricia to be off work. I didn't know her schedule, but if the wedding planning business was as busy as she said it was, then she'd be at work until at least five or six o'clock, probably even later.

I sat at the bar and ordered a scotch. My usual beer wasn't going to be enough after what I'd heard from Rebecca Acker. The bartender asked me if I wanted something to eat, perhaps my usual order, which was a burger topped with lettuce, onions, and avocado slices. I told her I should have been hungry since I hadn't eaten all day, but I wasn't, so I just stuck with the scotch, which quickly turned into two drinks. I thought about calling Foxx and asking him to join me, but I really wasn't ready to have a conversation with anyone.

Five o'clock eventually rolled around, and I drove the beige rental to Olivia's wedding planning company. Fortunately, there was a large window in the front of the business, and I could see Patricia working inside. I didn't see Olivia or any other person. I turned the car off and just watched her work for about an hour. From time to time, I'd turn the car back on and crank the air conditioning, but otherwise, I kept the window rolled down and spent my time thinking about the case. I knew there was probably no way I would ever have learned the Chambers' secret without Rebecca telling me, but now that she had, everything seemed so clear. It was really all right there, just sitting out in the open. I just had to confirm one more thing to be certain of all the players.

Patricia left the office about an hour later, and I followed her to a small grocery store a few blocks away. She was inside for no more than ten minutes. She left the store carrying two bags. Patricia climbed into her car and drove to a neighborhood in Ka'anapali. It wasn't that far from where I lived with Foxx. She parked in the driveway and carried the groceries to the front door. She pulled a key out of her front pocket and let herself inside.

It's never a good idea to judge a book by its cover, as they like to say, but I had a hard time believing Patricia could afford to either rent or own that house. The neighborhood was fairly exclusive and close to the beaches. I didn't know if she had family money like I did or not, but if so, why would she work as a personal assistant to Charlotte Chambers and then as another assistant to the granddaughter at a company that planned destination weddings?

I only had to wait another fifteen minutes to get my answer. A second car pulled into the driveway and parked beside Patricia's. Olivia got out of the car and walked to the front door. She also removed a key from her pocket and let herself in. Either the two ladies lived together, which seemed the likely answer, or one of them had given the other a key since they were such good friends, friends, by the way, who had only met a few weeks ago.

The blinds were closed on the front of the house, as all the houses in this neighborhood were fairly close together. Most houses on Maui were unless you had serious money and could afford to not be right on top of your next door neighbor.

I didn't think it would be possible for me to walk around to the side or back of the house without someone calling the police and reporting a suspected Peeping Tom. It wouldn't be the first time I'd been busted for that offense. Besides, I'd already gathered the information I wanted. Patricia and Olivia didn't just work together. They were good friends, maybe even something more.

I didn't feel like driving back to the airport and fetching my car, so I drove the rental back to Foxx's. Foxx was home, and I thanked him for watching Maui. I took the dog for a walk and thought about everything I'd learned that day. It was a hell of a lot of information, and I was still trying to put the pieces together. I got back to the house and grabbed a beer out of the refrigerator. I'd need to drink some water soon, and a lot of it.

The doorbell rang a few minutes after that. Maui took off running toward the front door. I followed him. I looked through the peephole and saw Alana. I opened the door. She looked upset.

"What's wrong?" I asked.

"I've been calling you all day," she said.

I reached into my front pocket and pulled out my phone. I hit the home button on the phone and saw it was turned off.

"That's right. I had to turn off my phone when I got on the plane."

"What plane?" she asked.

"Maybe you should come inside," I said.

I led Alana into the living room, and she and I sat down across from Foxx. I told them both about my trip to Oahu and the information I'd learned from Rebecca Acker. I also told them about following Patricia to the house in Ka'anapali and then seeing Olivia arrive at the same house.

"I'm sorry," Alana said.

"For what?" I asked.

"I made fun of you for spending the night going through all of Patricia's Facebook photos, but that's really what clued you in."

Alana's statement was only partially true. The only thing I'd known that morning was that something wasn't right, but I already knew that after the murder of Charlotte. It turns out the elderly lady I'd first met at Mara's office wasn't that much of a mystery at all. Charlotte's story was an old one. It was about greed and the willingness to look the other way to get the money and influence one wanted. Politicians did it every day. I shouldn't really be surprised that Charlotte did it too.

"Do you think Barry knows about this?" Alana asked.

I didn't answer Alana. I didn't know the answer.

20

THE FINAL INTERVIEW

ALANA CALLED MARA WINTERS THAT NIGHT TO ARRANGE A MEETING with Barry. Alana suggested we conduct the interview at his home or Mara's office instead of the police station. Mara recommended her office, so we met them there the next afternoon. Barry was already there by the time we arrived. I assumed he'd gotten there early to prepare with Mara. I had a feeling he already knew what we were going to ask him.

I thought Mara might object to my presence given that I wasn't any type of law enforcement official, but she didn't. Maybe she was worried she'd ruin what was left of our working relationship. I hadn't talked to her since she told Alana she needed to be present for all interviews regarding the Chambers family. Mara had hired me to find who was threatening Charlotte. In my mind, that job extended to discovering who had subsequently killed her, but Mara had switched directions on me when she moved to defending Charlotte's children. I knew she was in a tough position. There was no real evidence against any of them, and Mara certainly would have looked bad if she'd declined to represent them. The Chambers family was connected, and they could have easily damaged her reputation to other existing and potential clients. The rich have a way of sticking together.

Mara led us into her office. Barry was already inside, sitting on the sofa. He stood when we entered and shook hands with Alana and me. We all sat down, and Mara opened the conversation.

"So, Detective Hu, what did you want to speak to my client about?"

I interrupted her, as was our plan.

"Actually, do you mind if we wait a few minutes? I invited someone else to join us."

Technically, I had invited Olivia to the office, but it had been Alana's idea from the start. She didn't think she'd be able to get Olivia to admit to anything. I doubted I could either, especially after our last verbal sparring session. Alana thought, though, that she might lose her cool around her father, a man who was supposed to protect her but had failed to in spectacular fashion. There was also the potential of Barry getting angry when he heard Olivia's responses. Our plan was simple. Turn them against each other.

"Who are we waiting for?" Barry asked.

"Your daughter," I said.

Alana and I went silent while we let the panic build inside Barry. Olivia showed up five minutes later. Mara's assistant led her into the office. Olivia was smiling when she entered. She looked like she didn't have a care in the world. Alana, Mara, and I stood to greet her. Barry did not.

"Thank you for coming, Ms. Williams," Alana said, and they shook hands.

"You look familiar," Olivia said. She paused a moment. "Oh, yes, I have seen you before, on Mr. Rutherford's cell phone. He showed me a photo of you when he was in my office." Olivia turned to me. "You're right. She is quite beautiful."

Olivia smiled again, and we all sat down.

Alana turned to Barry. "I'm wondering, Mr. Williams, do you know Rebecca Acker?"

Barry shook his head. "I don't recall anyone by that name."

"Do you, Ms. Williams?" Alana asked.

"No."

"I'm sure you both know Edward Edelman's name," Alana said.

"No, I've never heard of him," Olivia said.

"He was Millard Chambers' original partner," Barry said. "I never met him, though. I believe he died years ago."

"Rebecca Acker was married to Mr. Edelman at one point. Mr. Rutherford here went to see her yesterday. She told him several interesting things," Alana said.

"What does any of this have to do with my clients?" Mara asked.

"It goes to the motive of Mrs. Chambers' murder," Alana said.

She waited for Barry or Olivia to say something, but they didn't. Mara didn't say anything, either.

"When did you know?" Alana asked Barry.

"Know what?" Barry asked.

"The answer to who killed your mother-in-law."

"I assure you if my client knew who murdered Mrs. Chambers, he would have immediately contacted the police," Mara said.

"Under normal circumstances, I would probably agree with you, but we all know that when it comes to matters of the family, doing the right thing can often be thrown out the door," Alana said.

I studied Olivia for her reaction. The smile was gone from her face, but she'd replaced it with a look of concern, not panic, mind you, but something that easily passed for sincere worry for her father. Her performance was magnificent, and I considered standing, applauding, and shouting, "Bravo!"

"Are you implying that Mr. Williams had something to do with the murder?" Mara asked.

"Not at all. But he knows who did it," Alana said.

"Did Bethany tell you, or did you figure it out on your own?" I asked.

"I don't know what you're talking about," Barry said.

"Did you know about what happened to your wife, or did she keep that to herself? I would understand if she kept it hidden. It wasn't her fault, but I'm sure she felt an amount of shame," Alana said.

Barry looked away, and I knew for certain that Bethany had told him.

"I would appreciate it if you would get to the point, Detective," Mara said.

"The man was despicable," Barry said, and he turned back to us. "I didn't know what he had done. I swear to you I didn't know. I never would have left her with him."

I continued to watch Olivia. She still had the look of sincere concern. There wasn't a trace of anger, and I was beginning to worry we'd fail.

"Why didn't you go to the police? The man had molested your daughter," Alana said.

"I wanted to, but Charlotte threatened us. She said Millard would be arrested, and the business would be ruined. She said we'd all be out on the street. I told her I didn't care. I told her I'd rather be on the street than see that man go free."

"What changed?" I asked.

Barry didn't answer.

"It's okay, Father. You can tell them," Olivia said.

Barry still didn't say anything.

"It was my mother," Olivia said. "She convinced him not to go. She said her father would never do it again. She said they needed to put it behind them and keep working at the hotel. It would be the family's security for the future."

"How do you know all of this?" Alana asked.

"My mother told me years later," Olivia said.

"Were you angry with her?" Alana asked.

"Of course," Olivia said.

I turned to Barry. "Bethany knew what was going on, didn't she? It had happened to her when she was a child," I said.

"I hated her for it," Barry admitted. "I actually took Olivia, and I left. Bethany and I were separated for a month, but she kept begging me to come back. She said it would never happen again. Olivia missed her mother. Charlotte came to see me while Bethany and I were separated. She told me that Bethany would have no choice but to file for divorce and the courts would give her primary custody. She said it made more sense for me to return, so I could be a constant presence in Olivia's life. I threatened to fight them in court, but she said the Chambers family had the money to outlast me, and they did."

Charlotte had worked it all out, I thought. She had put Barry into a no-win situation and gotten her way. It was all to protect the family legacy and their money.

"I told Mara this morning that I don't want any of it," Barry said.

"Any of what?" Alana asked.

"The inheritance. Bethany left me everything, but I'm giving it all to Olivia. Joe had no one to leave anything to, so half of his share would have gone to Bethany. I'll make sure Olivia gets those too."

"You're trying to buy Olivia's forgiveness?" I asked.

"No," Barry said.

"As regretful as all of this is, I still don't see what it has to do with Mrs. Chambers' death," Mara said.

"How long have you known Patricia?" I asked Olivia.

"Since my time in California. I met her while working on a music video production."

"She told me she'd only just met you at Charlotte's funeral and that conversation led to you offering her a job with your new company."

"Patricia is sometimes embarrassed by our relationship. It's true that society has come a long way, but she still feels uncomfortable talking about it. We lived together in L. A. She followed me to Maui when I decided to move back."

"So you were the one who introduced her to your grandmother?" Alana asked.

Olivia nodded. "My mother mentioned one day that my grandmother was looking for an assistant. I knew Patricia hadn't been able to find anything and was frustrated by that, so I recommended her."

"It was a convenient way to get her inside the house," I said.

"Why would I need to get her inside?"

"To learn things. To know her habits, where and when she went out, what she liked to eat and drink," Alana said.

"It was my grandmother's house. I could go over there anytime I wanted," Olivia said. "Or I could have simply asked her what I wanted to know."

"You're still not telling us how this relates to Charlotte's death," Mara said.

"The first two threatening letters were mailed. The third was delivered in person during the party. You managed to avoid suspicion by not being at the party and, therefore, not being there when the letter was left in the pantry. However, it would have been easy for Patricia to do it. She helped plan and set up the party. She had free rein of the house," Alana said.

"Since it was a party, I'd imagine lots of people had free rein of the house. Anyone could have left that letter, including my Uncle Joe." Olivia turned to me. "I already told you I thought he did it. He had a drug and alcohol problem. We all knew it. He even went so far as to forge a will and try to cheat my mother and uncle out of their rightful inheritances," Olivia said.

"Joe was nothing more than a distraction. You're right about the fake will and the drug problem. It was a desperate act from a desperate man, but it doesn't mean he killed his mother," Alana said.

"Are you going to accuse my clients of murdering Joe Chambers, too?" Mara asked.

"No, I think Joe's death was the accident it appeared to be," Alana said.

"Then there's the wine. You first wanted Charlotte's death to look like an accident. You took some of your mother's sleeping pills and had Patricia drop them in the bottle of wine," I said.

"That's ridiculous," Olivia said.

"You hated your grandmother for helping cover up the crime against you. I don't blame you. It was a despicable thing to do, but you also hated your mother. She of all people had to know the danger of leaving you with your grandfather, but she did it anyway. I don't know why she did. Maybe she was actually hoping it would happen so she wouldn't be alone in her misery," I said.

"That's not true," Olivia said.

"And what about your father? He was supposed to protect you," I said.

Olivia turned to Barry. "Would you like to answer that, Father?"

Barry said nothing. He didn't even look at her.

"You planned this entire thing out, Olivia. You set Patricia up inside. She delivered the third letter. She left the house early the day your grandmother was killed. That left Charlotte alone in the house for you to come over and murder her."

"I would never kill my grandmother. I loved her, despite what she did, and you're forgetting that no one forced my grandmother to be alone that day. Patricia told me my grandmother was the one who called off the security team."

"That's not exactly true. I spoke to the security company. I know the woman who worked on your grandmother's account. She said the person who called her and cancelled the service claimed to be Charlotte Chambers, but the voice was wrong. She said the voice sounded young, not someone who was over eighty," Alana said.

"That's hardly conclusive evidence, and it would get laughed out of court," Mara said.

"We think Patricia told Charlotte that you were behind the letters. Charlotte knew why, of course. No one needed to remind her of what had happened. She went to see you the day after the party, maybe to apologize, maybe to warn you off. Either way, I'm guessing she never thought you'd go through with your threats. She was wrong," I said.

"I'd barely seen my grandmother for weeks before she died. I was too busy at work. It's one of my biggest regrets. I certainly didn't see her the day she was killed," Olivia said.

"Did you know there's a security camera on the outside of the building across the street from yours? I got access to the footage. It clearly shows Charlotte arriving at your office and going inside," Alana said.

"So? That doesn't prove I was inside as well."

"Your car was already in the parking lot, and Charlotte didn't come out until ten minutes later."

"Again, that doesn't prove anything. I leave that office all the time to get a drink or go have lunch. She might have decided to wait for me. When I didn't return, she left," Olivia said.

"Do you always leave your business doors unlocked when you go out?" Alana asked.

"Sometimes. I'm forgetful. I'm very busy."

"It's not a crime for her to speak to her grandmother," Mara said.

"I didn't say it was, but you're conveniently ignoring the fact that she just lied to a police detective when she said she didn't see Charlotte that day," Alana said.

"No. All you established is that Charlotte went to her office," Mara said.

"Your mother knew you did it, didn't she?" I asked.

Olivia said nothing.

"You knew where your father kept his weapon," I continued. "I'm betting you offered her a choice, a bullet or the pills."

"Now you're accusing me of killing my mother, too?" Olivia asked.

"It explains why there weren't any prints on the handle of the gun. Someone had wiped them clean," Alana said.

"My mother's death was a suicide."

Alana turned to Barry. "Is that what you think?" He didn't answer.

"I hate to say this, but my mother was a deeply disturbed person. She was in therapy for many years and was addicted to those sleeping pills. Unfortunately, it wasn't a surprise when she took her own life."

"Is that true?" Alana asked Barry. "You told me the doctor had just prescribed those pills after Charlotte's funeral."

"My wife had just died. I didn't want to make her out to be an addict. Bethany had been taking pills for much longer. I tried to get her to stop, but she couldn't sleep without them."

"Tell her about the previous suicide attempt," Olivia urged her father.

Barry hesitated a moment, and then he said, "Bethany tried to kill herself after I took Olivia away. She overdosed on pills. Charlotte found her in the bathroom and had her rushed to the hospital."

"That doesn't mean she did it again," I said.

"What's more likely?" Olivia asked. "That I pointed a gun at my mother's head and forced her to take those pills or that she took her own life after a long history of mental problems and the recent depression over the loss of her mother and brother?"

"You know she killed your wife," I told Barry. "Are you going to just sit there and let her get away with it?"

That's exactly what he did, though. He said nothing. He did nothing. He didn't look at any of us. He just stared at the floor and retreated into his own little world of denial and despair.

"All you two have is guesswork. You have nothing that directly links either of my clients to either the death of Charlotte Chambers or Bethany Williams," Mara said.

She was right, unfortunately. Olivia had planned it perfectly, and she had a father who wasn't going to betray her. I doubted they'd come to any kind of official agreement. There probably hadn't been any conversation at all. She just knew he didn't have the guts to stand up for what was right. He hadn't done it when Olivia was molested by her grandfather. He certainly wasn't going to turn on his daughter now. This whole meeting had been a long shot at best. Alana and I knew that, but we had to try.

Mara ended the interview, and Alana and I stood to leave.

"Do you remember what I said to you in my office?" Olivia asked me.

"No, what did you say?"

"You're a clever man," Olivia nodded toward Alana, "and she's a beautiful woman, and I said not to let her get away."

I knew what Olivia was really saying. She was letting me know I had gotten it all right.

She was a hell of an actor, as I had pointed out earlier, and she was deeply disturbed like her mother. They were both victims of the same evil man, and the act of betrayal shaped both their destinies. Olivia had her innocence destroyed by her grandfather, and her grandmother had manipulated the situation to protect him, just as she had done when her daughter, Bethany, had been molested. Olivia's parents could have stepped up and protected her, but they didn't. Although I couldn't justify or condone the murders Olivia had committed, I could understand her desire for revenge.

The question now was, what would become of Olivia? Would she find peace now that those who betrayed her the most were gone, or would she fall deeper into a hole when the reality of what she had done finally seeped into her consciousness? And what of Barry? Would he seek revenge against his daughter by one day testifying against her? Probably not. At least that would be my bet, if I were a betting man.

21

DEFINING MOMENTS

SEVERAL DAYS WENT BY AFTER THE MEETING IN MARA'S OFFICE, AND I couldn't shake the feeling that I was wallowing in the filth of the Chambers family and wasn't able to wash myself clean. I decided I needed to get away. I asked Alana if she thought she could get a week off from work so we could take a trip. I thought she might take some convincing. She's a workaholic, whether she wants to admit it or not, so I was a little surprised when she immediately responded with the two-word answer "Hell, yes!"

The result of the Chambers case was a hard pill to swallow. I'd failed. It wasn't the first time in my life, and I knew with certainty it wouldn't be the last. The entire incident, if that's the right word, had left me feeling disgusted and sick. They were a family driven by greed, and a desire to preserve their riches meant they protected the guilty. Millard Chambers had been the lowest form of humanity I could think of. I remembered what his son, Mill, had told me the night of that party. His father had died on the golf course. Mill declared it as a great way to go out. The guy should have spent his final years rotting away in a prison. I did my best to push it all out of my mind, but it was impossible. I tried to concentrate on my upcoming trip with Alana. I planned every detail, every step, every moment in an effort to make it perfect. I knew it wouldn't be, though. Nothing is ever perfect, but I wanted it to be as close as possible. Just when I'd finally made some progress in pushing the Chambers family to the back of my mind, Mara called me.

"Hey, Poe, I just wanted to touch base with you and see how you were doing," she said.

"I'm fine. How are you?"

"Busy. But that's how things are normally around here."

"That's good, right?"

"I'm sorry for how things turned out," she said.

"So am I, but why are you apologizing? It wasn't your fault. You were just doing your job."

"I know, but I wish I could have done more to help."

"I get that, Mara. We're fine, though."

"Good, because I was hoping we could continue our working relationship."

"Did you have something new come up?" I asked.

"Not yet...but I will. Something always comes up."

"Why don't you call me when it does. We'll take each one as it comes, like we originally planned."

"In case you're interested, I heard Barry quit the Chambers Hotel. He sold his house and moved to Oahu. I don't know if he got a new job yet."

"You know, Mara, I don't mean to sound rude, but I don't care about the Chambers family anymore."

"I understand. I'll call you later then, when something comes up."

"Sure thing. Have a good day, Mara."

"You too."

I ended the call and slipped the phone back into my pocket. I hadn't been totally honest with Mara when I told her I didn't care anything about the Chambers family anymore. I kept myself apprised of Olivia's movements, hoping against hope that she'd slip up, but she was way too smart for that. I heard from the bartender at Harry's that Olivia was in the process of selling her wedding company and moving back to Los Angeles. If you'll recall, Patricia ate lunch on a regular basis at the bar, and she'd apparently been the one to tell the bartender this news. I wouldn't be surprised if she told the bartender just so I would eventually find out. Maybe it was their way of letting me know that I'd missed my chance. Of course, Patricia could be lying about moving to California. She'd done it before.

I also hadn't been honest with Mara when I'd implied there were no hard feelings between us. I was pretty pissed with her. I know it's an attorney's job to provide good counsel to their clients and make sure they receive a favorable outcome, but what about justice? What about doing the right thing? I wasn't sure how Mara could sleep knowing she had helped protect a corrupt family.

So why hadn't I told Mara I wasn't interested in working with her anymore? Two reasons, really. The first is that I don't like making decisions when I'm feeling emotional. I almost always regret it later. The second reason was that I'd become addicted to being involved with these cases. There was a certain high to chasing murderers and trying to outsmart them. I wouldn't be being honest with you, though, if I didn't admit that those feelings kind of freaked me out. It was a dangerous hobby I'd started, and I wasn't sure how it would end.

As for Charlotte's will, I assumed Mill got his half and Olivia got hers. I did read in the local news that Mill had negotiated a sales price for the hotel and property. Both Mill and Olivia were about to be very wealthy. I thought back to something Rebecca Acker told me in her office in Honolulu. She'd said it all started because she begged her father to give Edward Edelman the land for the Chambers Hotel. Now that land was selling for millions, and there wasn't one Edelman or one Acker that would see a dime.

So the case officially ended with riches and three deaths. Two of those deaths were murder, and no one would spend a single day in jail for them. Maybe Rebecca was right when she said there's no justice. I didn't want to believe that, but I was having a hard time thinking otherwise.

On the home front, Foxx finally admitted he was still seeing Hani. He wasn't sure, but he thought they might be dating exclusively. I asked him how he could not be certain, and he said the conversation never came up, but as far as he knew, neither of them were seeing anyone else. He then went into a long and detailed discussion on her talents in the bedroom and how he couldn't believe how amazing she looked naked. It was typical Foxx talk, but I won't share any more.

My trip with Alana ended on a much happier and upbeat note. I refused to tell her where we were going, but I did give her a breakdown of what the highs and lows of the temperature would be. She started to overpack because she didn't know the types of activities we would be doing. I told her to bring one small suitcase for her few items of clothing and a large empty suitcase for all the clothes she'd buy on the trip. I knew I was setting myself up for torture since I view shopping for clothes as one step above getting my fingernails violently ripped out.

We drove to the airport, and Alana still had no idea where we were headed until I handed her the boarding passes after we checked in.

"Paris!" she exclaimed, and I thought the normally cool and calm Alana was going to jump in my arms.

For those of you who have read my previous two tales, you know I have horrible luck when it comes to air travel. I normally get stuck near the back of the plane, if not the very last row in front of the toilet. I believe the airlines think my middle name is "middle-seat-on-the-plane."

The flight plan called for a five-hour trip to San Francisco, a rather long layover in the airport, and then an incredibly long flight to Paris. I didn't think I'd be in one piece if I flew economy. Plus, I hoped this would be a memorable event, so I had decided to spring for two first-class tickets. The price was obscene, and I thoroughly cursed the greed of the airline as I typed my Visa number into the checkout box on the travel website.

Alana was floored when she saw where we were sitting. The drinks were free, and the food was several notches above the food you get in the back of the plane, but that still wasn't saying much considering I wouldn't feed that garbage to Maui the dog. The biggest advantage of first class revealed itself when it came time to try to sleep. The seats actually reclined until they were completely horizontal. It was the first time in dozens of flights that I was actually able to sleep on a plane.

I'd rented us a room in a boutique hotel a few blocks from the Champs-Elysees. The room was small but comfortable, pretty typical for a European hotel. We spent the first day touring the Eiffel Tower and the Arc de Triomphe. The second day was almost one hundred percent shopping on the Champs-Elysees. Alana bought so many new clothes that I realized I should have suggested she bring two empty suitcases. The third and fourth days were dedicated to museums. We toured the Louvre and the Musee d'Orsay. Call me crazy, but I actually enjoyed the latter more. The Louvre was a bit overcrowded and chaotic. Okay, it was a lot overcrowded and chaotic.

The meals were a bit hit or miss. We did our best to search reviews online and get the advice of the concierge at the hotel, but we still struck out a couple of times.

All things considered, we had the time of our lives. At one point, Alana asked me if this was what my European trips had been like with my parents. I told her we saw many of the same things, but it was a lot different going back to the hotel with a beautiful woman.

As much fun as I was having, I was also suffering from a lot of anxiety. I know that sounds like a weird combination of emotions, but that's how it was for me. Why? Well, there was the little thing of the engagement ring in my pocket.

Ironically enough, I'd taken Olivia's advice and bought a ring with an Asscher-cut diamond. I almost pulled it out on the third night, but I found that my hand was shaking so badly and I didn't want to embarrass myself in front of Alana. I decided the next morning that I would pop the question that night. Big mistake. I got myself so worked up throughout the day that I thought I might faint as we finished dinner. I'm sure you're laughing at me by now. I don't blame you. It was kind of pathetic.

We toured the Latin Quarter and Notre Dame on the fifth day. That night we had dinner near the Louvre at a ridiculously overpriced restaurant, but the food was delicious. We decided to walk back to the hotel since the weather was so nice.

There's a beautiful park you walk through to get from the Louvre to the Champs-Elysees. I'm sure it's got a name, but I don't remember what it is. The park was so lovely that we sat down on a bench so we could look at this little pond surrounded by statues.

As we sat there and watched the people walk by, I realized I'd come to another defining moment. Although this one was infinitely more interesting than whether to tell a chain-restaurant manager to take a leap or whether I wanted an investigative career catching cardiac surgeons cheating on their wives.

Yes, this one was vastly more important. Did I ask or did I not? And what of Alana? Would she say yes or would she say no? It was a simple question, really. It doesn't get much easier than yes or no.

I ran my hand over my front pocket and felt the bump of the ring. I must have repeated that action a million times since we'd gotten to Paris, praying each time that it hadn't fallen out.

"I don't know if I could ever see myself leaving Maui, but if I did, I could see myself here," Alana said.

"There's a good reason this city has attracted so many great artists."

"How many times have you been here?" Alana asked.

"This is my fifth time," I said, "but I never get tired of it."

"It's so beautiful," she said.

I laughed.

"What's so funny?"

"I was just thinking back to the first time I met you. I couldn't believe I'd just stepped on your toes at that art show."

"It wasn't a smooth move," Alana admitted.

"That night you came over to Foxx's house for the first time, did you ever think we'd end up here, sitting on a bench in Paris and looking at the night sky?" I asked.

"No. That wasn't what I was thinking that night."

"What were you thinking?" I asked.

"I was trying to decide whether or not to arrest you for interfering in police business."

I nodded. "I'm glad you didn't," I said.

Now it was Alana's turn to laugh. "I'd doubt you would have wanted to take me to Paris if I'd tossed you in jail."

"I don't know. I might have gotten around to forgiving you. Plus, I probably deserved it. I was interfering."

We watched people walk by for several more minutes. Neither of us said a word. We just enjoyed each other's company and the beautiful scenery.

I stood, but Alana stayed sitting on the park bench.

The defining moment. To ask or not to ask.

Would she say yes or would she say no?

I got down on one knee and pulled the ring out of my pocket.

"Detective Hu, I've never met anyone quite as beautiful and remarkable as you. I love you. Would you do me the honor of being my wife?"

She smiled and said, "Yes."

THE END

~

Are you ready for more in the Murder on Maui Mystery series?

Poe's next mystery, **Hot Sun Cold Killer**, is available now!

An old murder. A new threat. Can Poe find the killer before it's too late?

Edgar Allan "Poe" Rutherford is Maui's best unlicensed private investigator. When a client asks Poe to look into a decade-old death on the beach, he can't help but be intrigued. The police ruled it a suicide, but it's up to him to prove otherwise.

As soon as Poe takes the case, people related to the victim start turning up dead--a sure sign that he's on the right track. But can Poe identify the killer... before he becomes the next victim?

Hot Sun Cold Killer is the fourth standalone novel in a series of clever mysteries set in paradise. If you like colorful characters, witty humor, and warm sand between your toes, then you'll love Robert W. Stephens' Murder on Maui series.

ALSO BY ROBERT W. STEPHENS

Murder on Maui Mystery Series

If you like charismatic characters, artistic whodunnits, and twists you won't see coming, then you'll love this captivating mystery series.

Aloha Means Goodbye (Poe Book 1)

Wedding Day Dead (Poe Book 2)

Blood like the Setting Sun (Poe Book 3)

Hot Sun Cold Killer (Poe Book 4)

Choice to Kill (Poe Book 5)

Sunset Dead (Poe Book 6)

Ocean of Guilt (Poe Book 7)

The Tequila Killings (Poe Book 8)

Wave of Deception (Poe Book 9)

The Last Kill (Poe Book 10)

Mountain of Lies (Poe Book 11)

Rich and Dead (Poe Book 12)

Poe's First Law (Poe Book 13)

Poe's Justice (Poe Book 14)

Poe's Rules (Poe Book 15)

Alex Penfield Supernatural Mystery Thriller Series

If you like supernatural whodunnits, gripping actions, and heroes with a troubled past, then you'll love this series.

Ruckman Road (Penfield Book 1)

Dead Rise (Penfield Book 2)

The Eternal (Penfield Book 3)

Nature of Darkness (Penfield Book 4)

The Eighth Order (Penfield Book 5)

Ruckman Road

To solve an eerie murder, one detective must break a cardinal rule: never let the case get personal...

Alex Penfield's gunshot wounds have healed, but the shock remains raw. Working the beat could be just what the detective needs to clear his head. But when a corpse washes up on the Chesapeake Bay, Penfield's first case back could send him spiraling...

As Penfield and his partner examine the dead man's fortress of a house, an army of surveillance cameras takes the mystery to another level. When the detective sees gruesome visions that the cameras fail to capture, he begins to wonder if his past has caught up with him. To solve the murder, Penfield makes a call on a psychic who may or may not be out to kill him...

His desperate attempt to catch a killer may solve the case, but will he lose his sanity in the process?

Ruckman Road is the start of a new paranormal mystery series featuring Detective Alex Penfield. If you like supernatural whodunnits, gripping action, and heroes with a troubled past, then you'll love Robert W. Stephens' twisted tale.

Standalone Dark Thrillers

Nature of Evil

Rome, 1948. Italy reels in the aftermath of World War II. Twenty women are brutally murdered, their throats slit and their faces removed with surgical precision. Then the murders stop as abruptly as they started, and the horrifying crimes and their victims are lost to history. Now over sixty years later, the killings have begun again. This time in America. It's up to homicide detectives Marcus Carter and Angela Darden to stop the crimes, but how can they catch a serial killer who leaves no traces of evidence and no apparent motive other than the unquenchable thirst for murder?

The Drayton Diaries

He can heal people with the touch of his hand, so why does a mysterious group want Jon Drayton dead? A voice from the past sends Drayton on a desperate journey to the ruins of King's Shadow, a 17th century plantation house in Virginia that was once the home of Henry King, the wealthiest and most powerful man in North America and who has now been lost to time. There, Drayton meets the beautiful archaeologist Laura Girard, who has discovered a 400-year-old manuscript in the ruins. For Drayton, this partial journal written by a slave may somehow hold the answers to his life's mysteries.

ABOUT THE AUTHOR

Robert W Stephens is the author of the Murder on Maui series, the Alex Penfield novels, and the standalone thrillers The Drayton Diaries and Nature of Evil.

You can find more about the author at robertwstephens.com.

Visit him on Facebook at facebook.com/robertwaynestephens

ACKNOWLEDGMENTS

Thanks to you readers for investing your time in reading my story. I hope you enjoyed it. Poe, Alana, Foxx, and Maui will return.